AJAY AND THE
JAIPUR MOON

VARSHA SHAH

Chicken House

2 Palmer Street, Frome, Somerset BA11 1DS
www.chickenhousebooks.com

Text © Varsha Shah 2023
Illustration © Sònia Albert 2023

First published in Great Britain in 2023
Chicken House
2 Palmer Street
Frome, Somerset BA11 1DS
United Kingdom
www.chickenhousebooks.com

Chicken House/Scholastic Ireland, 89E Lagan Road, Dublin Industrial Estate,
Glasnevin, Dublin D11 HP5F, Republic of Ireland

Cover and interior design by Helen Crawford-White
Typeset by Dorchester Typesetting Group Ltd
Printed and bound in Great Britain by CPI Group (UK) Ltd, Croydon CR0 4YY

FSC
www.fsc.org
MIX
Paper | Supporting
responsible forestry
FSC® C171272

1 3 5 7 9 10 8 6 4 2

British Library Cataloguing in Publication data available.

PB ISBN 978-1-915026-13-2
eISBN 978-1-915026-47-7

To Zoë, Gavin, Oscar, Tilly and M.S.L.S

and

Bob, Chris and Savannah

*It is the bright day that
brings forth the adder . . .*

WILLIAM SHAKESPEARE

Julius Caesar

Act II, Scene I

1

A warm breeze whirled through the station, catching and whipping up a page from the last copy of *The Mumbai Sun* and blowing it along the railway platform. Ajay chased it down, ducking past the railway guard blowing his whistle, around a woman in a midnight-blue sari glittering with tiny mirrors, and through two boys, playing with plastic rockets, to catch it.

Another gust and it would sweep up out of reach!

Ajay dived, just as it was about to blow upwards and away, and caught it with his free hand like one of India's cricketing fielders at their best.

Ajay held up the faluda-pink paper in triumph

(although sadly, no one else seemed to have noticed his amazing feat of skill and dexterity). Breathing heavily, he dusted himself off, looking around as he folded and smoothed the page back into shape over the rest of the paper. It was evening – there wasn't much time left to sell the last copy. Bathed in the silvery light that spilt from the open roof, the last clanking trains were leaving the station, the bustling crowds of commuters were eager to get home, and the hawkers were closing up their tiffin boxes of fried round puris and hot pepper curry.

'Utter garbage. Should have let it fly off!'

Ajay turned. Another customer! He smiled winningly at the bald-headed businessman who had spoken, and who was now returning Ajay's smile with a look of utter distaste.

Ajay was not disheartened. After all, he was not just a twelve-year-old (or thereabouts) railway kid now. He was the editor of *The Mumbai Sun*!

'Ten rupees to buy *The Mumbai Sun* – the paper that brought down a corrupt billionaire, saved a slum and that I, myself,' Ajay added modestly, 'am the editor of.'

The bald-headed businessman snorted. 'All of that's in the past. I want to know – what's in it today?'

Ajay felt his spirits drop. Everything they had done was yesterday's news already! Then he rallied. 'We have new cartoons by *The Mumbai Sun* illustrator, Yasmin.' (Yasmin was also about twelve, lived in the slum and was Ajay's best friend.) 'We have recipes from the Secret Cook, Vinod, who now has his own food stall at the station. And we have cricketing news of Jai, the kid from the slum and the best batter in all of Mumbai!'

He waited for the businessman to be impressed.

The businessman looked down at him, a smirk across his face. 'Let me give you some free advice. People of substance aren't interested in what happens to people like you. All they want is information that will help them get rich. How to invest in the projects of billionaires – like Mrs Surya's private Space Programme for instance.' There was a crafty look in his eye. 'I don't suppose you have any inside knowledge to share?'

Ajay felt *The Mumbai Sun* crumple in his hand.

All that anyone in Mumbai – in fact anyone in the whole of India – was talking about was the billionaire Mrs Surya, her company, WECU, and the WECU Space Programme which was building a rocket to go to the moon. All that anyone wanted was more news of it. He really should be over the moon (so to speak) at the sudden demand for newspapers.

There was just one problem.

The Space Programme was TOP SECRET. Even Mr Gupta, Ajay's friend and editor of *The City Paper*, had been denied access. There was no way that Ajay and his friends, kids who had been abandoned on the railways or who lived in the slums, would be able to get in.

And no news of the Space Programme would soon mean no newspapers sold.

The bald-headed businessman's train clanged and hissed as it rattled up to the platform.

There was no more time.

Ajay shook his head sadly.

The businessman laughed. 'I should have known that a newspaper run by railway rats wouldn't be able to find real stories!'

Ajay rallied. 'I don't have inside knowledge, but I do have something better.' He looked around, and then motioned the businessman to bend down. Ajay whispered in his ear.

The businessman's eyes became wider. He jumped up. 'A ticket to space! A chance to be like other billionaires. A chance to look down on Earth and all the people left on it.' He snatched at the paper. 'Give me that!'

'Ten rupees,' said Ajay firmly, holding it to one side.

The businessman tossed over the money, grabbing the paper out of Ajay's hand and tearing it apart until he found the page he was looking for. His face turned bright orange. 'What is this?' he said, holding out the page that had inked on it, 'Free ticket to Space (and a Rocket samosa on the presentation of this coupon!)'.

Ajay waved in the direction of the stall being manned by Vinod. 'It is the name of the Secret Cook's food stall.' He coughed and put on a deep voice. 'Space: A place that will take you out of this world, sizzle your senses and make you see the world differently.' Ajay paused, nodding for extra emphasis. He felt very proud of the slogan – he'd come up with it with tears flowing down his face after eating half of one of Vinod's extra-spicy samosas.

The bald-headed businessman's face turned a deeper shade of orange. 'Why you little—'

Ajay quickly stepped out of the way. 'You'd better hurry – or you'll miss your train!' said Ajay, pointing as the businessman's train started to roll out of the station on its heavy, clattering wheels.

The businessman looked at the train, at Ajay, and then back at the train – and started to run.

As the train left, with the businessman on it, waving a clenched fist at him, Ajay waved back.

It was a shame that the businessman hadn't been able to get to Space that evening, but it would always be there waiting for him.

And in the meantime . . . Ajay rummaged in his pocket, found the remaining half of the super-spicy Rocket samosa, and bit into it, tears flooding his face.

2

With the last copy of *The Mumbai Sun* sold (and the rest of the samosa eaten), Ajay was sitting on a bench on the railway platform. He tossed one of the silver coins the bald-headed businessman had given him up into the air, watched it spin in the moonlight, caught it, and tossed it again.

There had to be some way of getting access to Mrs Surya's Space Programme!

Ajay looked up at the full moon, shining like a great silver orb in the sky. When he was younger, and had recently been abandoned on the station platform by his mother with only her gold-nib fountain pen, he had been drawn to the moon as to a friend. Alone and shivering with cold, he had imagined that his mother was somewhere in Mumbai, looking up at the same moon, thinking about him and wishing she were with him – opening her mouth to say—

'Ajay!'

Ajay blinked. Those were not the sweet tones he remembered his mother having.

'Ajay!'

It was Saif, who, like Ajay, was also about twelve. As Saif stormed up the platform, he did not look happy. Ajay shook himself free from his daydreams. He had been avoiding his friend all day, but Saif had caught him now, fair and square.

'Saif—' Ajay began, placatingly.

Saif put up his hand. 'Do not "Saif" me!' he said. 'Look!' He held out his hands, palm side up.

Obligingly, Ajay looked. There were marks of engine oil on them, but otherwise they seemed much the same as always. He opened his mouth to say so, but Saif, whose cheeks were flushed with indignation, spoke over him.

'Do you not see? The calluses? The bruises? The suffering? I am an apprentice engineer! I need delicate hands to be able to do fine work. And instead I am hurting them? Why? Because instead of a printer, we are using a hand roller – *a hand roller* – to print copies and copies of *The Mumbai Sun*!'

Ajay sighed. He knew using a hand roller to print the paper was exhausting and tiring for all of them, even though they took it in turns.

But printing presses cost money.

Ajay opened up his pockets with the day's takings, knelt and spilt the coins on to the platform to count them. It did not take long.

'Well?' said Saif.

Ajay swallowed. 'It's not quite enough, brother Saif.'

In fact, there were barely enough coins for food (his stomach growled in agreement – one samosa a day was not enough), never mind the vast sum needed to buy a printing press. To make money they needed to make more copies; to make more copies they needed to buy a printing press; to buy a printing press they needed money; and to make money . . . got them right back where they started.

And that was if anyone wanted to read the

news they wrote in the first place.

Ajay had sold the small number of copies they had been able to print today, but as they got closer and closer to Mrs Surya's rocket launch, would anyone even look at *The Mumbai Sun* if it did not contain news of the Space Programme?

He felt defeated. It would take a miracle to get into the Top-Secret Headquarters of Mrs Surya's WECU Space Programme – and railway and street kids were lucky if they just managed to survive. They did not get miracles.

'Ajay, look!' Saif was grabbing on to his arm, jumping with excitement.

Ajay looked up, just like everyone else on the platform, and gasped.

Streaking across the sky, past the moon, burning as it tore high over them, was a dark blot.

It hurtled closer and closer to them, edged in flames.

Splitting the sky in half, the flames turned bright orange, then fierce gold and then, finally, crackling, blazing silver.

The sky was awash in shimmering light.

And then, all of a sudden, as if a lamp had been

switched off, the light was extinguished . . .

. . . and the sky turned dark again!

Cries of awe and terror filled Ajay's ears.

'What was that?' Saif whispered, waving his arms upwards at the night sky.

Dazzled, Ajay shook his head. For a moment he had been blinded by the light. He fought to catch his breath.

Suddenly, all around them phones were beeping with notifications. Commuters were rapidly scrolling through them, their eyes glazed, their faces reflecting the glare of the screens.

Ajay grabbed Saif's arm, pulling him along as he raced back inside the station, and pushed through the crowd to get close to the big screen that had recently been installed there for the passengers. Niresh, the tall station attendant and Ajay's good friend, waved a greeting as he changed the channels with a remote.

'*We interrupt this programme with news from a very special press conference.*'

Ajay felt his eyes become bigger. There on the screen was Mrs Surya, owner of the private Space Programme, WECU, dressed in black trousers, a black top and a black sleek jacket that looked as if it were made of butter. She was wearing a silver pin displaying the WECU logo: an eye over a horizontal dagger. Next to her, smiling, was Mrs Shania, the politician with a beehive hairdo and red nails, known as 'Mother of the City'. Mrs Surya was speaking. 'This is a great day. A fireball has just been seen shooting across India's skies. To commemorate our first planned rocket launch, I will pay an incredible cash prize to whoever finds the meteorite first, and allow exclusive access to the WECU Space Programme's top-secret headquarters!'

There was a spontaneous cheer from the other people in the station, and an eruption of chattering.

'What does this mean, Ajay?' said Saif, still panting as he turned to look at him.

Ajay grinned.

He stood up to his full height (which was *still* shorter than the other railway kids) feeling excitement bursting inside him like jet fuel. 'It means, brother Saif, that we just got our miracle – the chance to buy a printing press *and* tell the story about the rocket blasting to the moon!'

3

It was later that night. Ajay looked around the engine room. The whole team had gathered there, and the lamplight was flickering ghoulishly over their faces, throwing moving shadows around the room. Vinod, one of the older railway kids – tall, lanky, gentle and quiet – was plating up. Luckily there were some leftovers from his food stand.

Ajay, ignoring the increased growling of his stomach, coughed importantly and began to speak. 'As you all know, *The Mumbai Sun* has been in some difficulty.'

'The printing press,' piped up Saif, showing off his hands to the others.

'But we now have a plan. We are going to find the meteorite that has crashed somewhere in India, collect the prize money that Mrs Surya has promised and get the space story of the century!'

Ajay waited for applause, but his statement was greeted with shocked silence.

It was Yasmin, looking tired from the sewing jobs she had been doing to make a few rupees, who spoke first – her green eyes baffled. 'And how exactly are we going to do that?'

Saif bustled his way to the table, carrying a large map which he proceeded to open up, using Jai's cricket bat to hold down one edge and the lamp to hold down the other. It was a map of India, criss-crossed with railway lines, that Ajay recognized from Niresh's office.

'I sent out word through the slums across Mumbai and among the railway kids asking for sightings of the meteor,' began Saif. 'I then plotted each sighting.'

Ajay burst into applause! Hundreds of slum and railway kids had answered the call – the Indian Space Research Organization itself wouldn't have been able to collect information on so many sightings in one night!

'I then made several calculations,' continued Saif, 'using mathematical models, mechanical tools and engineering devices to track the meteor's trajectory. And, taking several factors into account, I believe that the meteorite has landed somewhere near here.' He jabbed at the map.

Jai, who at fifteen was the oldest of them all, looked at where Saif's finger had landed, then up – the lamplight turning his eyes into liquid gold. 'The Indian Ocean?'

'What?' Saif looked at where he was pointing, and hastily moved his finger. 'I mean – here.' He jabbed at the map again, a bit less dramatically.

'Jaipur?' said Vinod, passing around the plates.

Ajay nodded, grabbing the plate of dhokra as it went past. 'The Pink City. According to Saif's calculations, the meteorite has landed somewhere close to the city. We just need to go and find it.'

'But Ajay, even if Saif is right—' began Yasmin.

'Of course I am right,' interrupted Saif, affronted. 'I am an apprentice engineer. I have made clear and correct calculations.'

'Even *though* Saif is right,' Yasmin corrected

16

herself. 'How are we going to afford the railway tickets? To get there, we have to travel up to Rajasthan. We can't get there without going by train.'

They all looked at Ajay. He tried to sound confident. 'We have some coins we have collected from the sale of the newspapers—'

'That won't be enough,' said Yasmin with certainty. Ajay sighed. He should have known he couldn't fool her.

Jai pushed his hand through his hair in frustration. 'I wish I was bringing in more money. The team and I are playing more and more matches, but . . .' He left the rest of the sentence unsaid, but Ajay could guess. The cricket team from the slum had fought for – and got – recognition, although it had lost a recent match against a team from Calcutta. However, whilst some big shots were making huge amounts of profit selling tickets to watch them, the team itself was barely making anything.

'I could try and bring more in as well,' said Vinod, his face looking pinched.

Ajay shook his head. 'You do enough, bringing

us the leftovers. We'd starve if it wasn't for—'

Ajay stopped and stared at Vinod with a sudden flash of understanding. The 'leftovers' that Vinod brought every few evenings weren't leftovers at all, but Vinod's contribution to the team. No wonder, despite being the best cook in Mumbai (as voted for by 'The Canary', Mumbai's most respected food critic!), Vinod was still paying for his wooden food stall each week rather than being able to buy it outright.

Yasmin crossed her arms. 'I could—'

'Stop!' Ajay straightened and looked them all in the eye. 'I told you. I have a plan! I will get the tickets to Jaipur. Vinod, you bring food for the journey; Saif – the navigational instruments we need to narrow the search to find the meteorite once we're in Jaipur; Jai and Yasmin, speak to all your friends from the slum and see if they have any contacts in Jaipur. We will all meet at the railway platform at six in the morning exactly. Agreed?'

There was a pause. Then, slowly, everyone nodded (even Jai, who hated early mornings), confidence in Ajay glowing warm in their eyes.

Only Yasmin was frowning slightly.

Ajay smiled. 'Then let's finish the food.'

One by one Yasmin, Saif, Vinod and Jai all took their plates and started eating, and gradually the tension eased and anticipation of the trip began. Ajay bit hungrily into the fried piece of dhokra he had taken, crunching the nubbly edges and then dipping the soft centre into a sauce of fresh tomatoes spiced with chilli and salt, trying to make the one piece last. It was only when he had finished, and everyone else was engrossed in their own conversations, that he let his thoughts hit him like a hammer.

Just how was he going to get those train tickets – the tickets he needed to win the treasure hunt and save *The Mumbai Sun*?

4

Ajay waited until Jai and Yasmin had gone back to the slum and Vinod and Saif were fast asleep (Saif had been snoring loudly and was now happily sleep-talking about samosas), before rolling out from under the bench on the station platform. The air was sharp with cold, the sky was powdery with stars and the moon was shining brightly. For a moment, Ajay looked up at it, hope and fear churning inside him. If only the moon were really made of silver, rather than moon dust! Mrs Surya's rocket could mine it, bringing back enough wealth to make all the people in all the slums of Mumbai millionaires. He and his friends would never need to worry about money again.

Ajay gritted his teeth and brought his focus back to Earth. He didn't need to be a millionaire – he just needed enough money to save his newspaper! He tiptoed his way out of the station and then began to run through the streets of Mumbai. Even at night, Mumbai was packed – with beeping lorries, zipping rickshaws, and bellowing cows whose large dark eyes, long lashes and pale white hides glowed softly in the moonlight. He ran through the markets, where vats of oil were still sizzling; on the edges of the slum, where dogs were barking loudly at stray cats that hissed back at them; and into the hush of one of the wealthiest districts in Mumbai.

Ajay came to a stop outside The Antique Shop. Even from the outside, it looked expensive – the lamps in the windows were still lit, glittering over wedding necklaces, lockets and silver fountain pens. Ajay felt his mouth gape at the high prices they were listed for. Just the sale of one would feed him and his friends for a year!

He took a deep breath and knocked on the door.

No answer.

Had he got it wrong? He was sure this was the right place – the place that people from the slum talked about with dark hopeless shadows in their eyes, when there was no other way out. And it wasn't yet closing time, he was sure of that. Growing up in the shadow of the station clock meant that even without wearing watches all the railway kids could always tell what time it was, to the minute.

He knocked again, louder this time.

The door swung open. A man in an expensive-looking suit, with a handkerchief in his top pocket and very white teeth, looked out with a big smile.

Ajay coughed. The man looked down. The smile was instantly wiped from the man's face, as if by a windscreen wiper.

'A slum kid! What are you doing here?' the man said furiously.

What if he'd been wrong? What if there was no way to get the railway tickets? Ajay straightened his spine. 'I had heard that this was the place to borrow money.'

The man looked even angrier. 'This is the

entrance for customers! You don't come in through here!'

Before Ajay could say what he thought of that, the man had picked him up by the scruff of his neck and dragged him inside the shop. Ajay had the impression of chandeliers that sparked rainbows of light, warm air scented with musk and a slick marble floor, before he was pushed through the doors at the back of the shop, down a small corridor and into a dark, strangely cold room that had cracks on the walls.

'Wait here,' the man with the handkerchief barked. 'Mr Soni is sitting over there. He will see you when he's ready.' The man turned on his heels and powered through the doors back into the front of the shop.

Ajay dusted himself off. In the corner, at a table with a cash register, was a young man wearing a glittering, expensive-looking diamond-and-gold watch.

'Well?' said Mr Soni briskly, the lamplight flickering over him.

Ajay was silent.

'Do you have anything?'

Ajay steeled himself. He had no other choice. He had to bet everything on one roll of the dice – and that meant getting to Jaipur on the next available train; the train usually used by tourists. Slowly, from behind his ear where he always kept it, he took out the fountain pen, with the black scrolled barrel and golden nib – the only thing his mother had left him when she had abandoned him at the railway station. The nib caught the light, just like it had all those years ago.

Ajay's heart stopped.

He couldn't give the pen away – even for a short while! It was all he had of her. He could no more give it away than he could give away his heart.

Ajay jumped off the chair, his hand holding the fountain pen so tightly to his chest that his knuckles shone white.

Mr Soni laughed. 'It is always the way. You lot come here seeking money, then you feign reluctance.' He came closer, and the lamplight was reflected like a little red flame in his watch. 'Come. Think about it. What choice do you have except to give the pen as security? It is not like the banks will give you money.'

Ajay felt sick.

He stretched out his arm, his hand trembling as he opened it to show the pen. Mr Soni's eyes gleamed as he picked up the pen and quickly examined it with his eyeglass. He put it to one side and took out a little silver money clip, before extracting three notes and placing them in Ajay's hand.

'How do I get it back?' Ajay asked, his voice wavering. Without his mother's pen, he felt like he was suddenly missing a limb.

Mr Soni's mouth was still curved in a smile. 'You pay the sum, and interest, back in a week's time. If you fail to pay it . . . well,' he paused, then said with relish, 'we get to keep the pen.'

Ajay's hand tightened over the notes that Mr Soni had given him.

He watched as Mr Soni pushed his diamond-encrusted watch back up on his wrist. The light from the stones glittered straight into Ajay's eyes.

'I'll pay – and get it back,' Ajay said, clenching his fists.

'That's what you all say.'

Ajay leant forward. 'Mr Soni?' he said quietly.

'Yes?'

'How much is the watch that you're wearing?'

Mr Soni laughed. 'Why? Don't tell me you want to buy one? You might as well wish for the moon. This watch is worth more than you will earn in your entire lifetime – you *and* all your friends in the slum put together.'

Ajay looked at him gravely. 'That is a shame.'

Mr Soni's face went still.

'Your watch is behind. By three minutes.' Ajay let his words sink in, then added brightly, 'But do not worry, Mr Soni. In the slum we have good watch repairers. They won't even charge you much because they'll feel sorry for you.'

Mr Soni's mouth opened, but no words came out.

Ajay took a moment to appreciate the effect. Then he walked out of the shop clutching the three notes to his chest.

It was only when he got outside, in the cool night air, reaching automatically behind his ear for his mother's fountain pen and remembering that it was no longer there, that he sank to his knees in the shadows.

For the first time, he wanted to hide away from the moon's light. It glared down at him, reproach-fully.

5

The next morning, pushing the ache at the loss of his mother's pen to the back of his heart, Ajay looked around in awe. So this was what it was like for them all to be in a first-class carriage on a luxurious train to Jaipur! Ajay bounced experimentally on the seat – his eyes widening as he sprang up. No hard wooden seats here! The glass windows of the carriage were frosted and etched, the wood shone with a caramel sheen, and the white tablecloths and silver cutlery sparkled in the rose dawn light. Yasmin was sitting opposite him, following the thread of copper embroidery looping in a jasmine flower on the emerald-green armrest with her finger.

She looked up at Ajay, her eyes shining. 'This is beautiful.' Then she frowned as she stared at his ear. 'Where's your fountain pen?'

'I left it with Mr Sandhu at the stationery stall for safekeeping,' said Ajay, crossing his fingers behind his back. Telling the lie he felt, for a moment, just so alone. But he must have sounded convincing because Yasmin relaxed back into her seat.

'Where are the other passengers?' Jai whispered, spinning the cricket bat in his hand nervously.

Glad for the distraction, Ajay craned his neck, looking up and down and sideways. It was a good question. It would have cost Niresh his job to get them free tickets (Ajay, unknown to the rest of the team, had insisted on paying for them). Niresh had, however, been able to upgrade them due to a last-minute cancellation. Yet even with all its tickets booked, the carriage wasn't a tenth full compared to the carriages further down the train. And it was very quiet. The few passengers he could see – all dressed in sharp suits, silk saris and embroidered dresses, and speaking in soft, hushed tones – could be diplomats, murderers or even spies! Ajay beamed. This was the dream of an undercover journalist – he and the others could put on disguises, blend into the background, be discreet, quietly discover the passengers' secrets . . .

'Ajay, I am here!' Saif shouted from the door to the carriage, panting as he dragged an enormous, rattling, bulging suitcase that Ajay had seen gathering dust in the lost property office. There were squeals and the angry shaking out of newspapers as the suitcase rolled over feet, knocked into elbows and hit seat rests. Every passenger, including those across the aisle, a powerfully built man in a light-grey suit and silver tiepin, and two tourists with two flashy cameras, turned to glare at them in his wake.

Ajay sighed.

'Do you need all of this?' asked Vinod, astonished, as Saif reached them.

Saif scrambled up on his seat, holding the handle of the suitcase protectively. 'I am an apprentice engineer! How am I to work without proper equipment? You did not expect me to travel without all the metal-working tools I need to make astronomical instruments? I need to chart the skies of Jaipur and plot against them the sightings of the meteor.'

'But do you need *all* your tools?' asked Vinod, trying to find room for his feet.

Saif nodded. 'How do I know in advance which ones will be necessary? This way I am prepared for every possibility.'

It was impossible to argue with that.

'After all,' continued Saif, holding court, 'an apprentice engineer without his tools would be like Ajay without his fountain pen.' Saif airily pointed at Ajay, then blinked and looked closer at Ajay's ear. 'Where *is* your fountain pen, Ajay?'

'With Mr Sandhu,' repeated Ajay, telling the lie more easily this time.

Saif nodded.

There was a cough above them. A waiter stood there with a starched uniform. 'I am terribly sorry,' he said, speaking to Saif, 'but would it be at all possible to ask you to relocate and reposition your bag, please, as it is causing an obstruction to the breakfast cart?'

Saif looked at Ajay in confusion.

'He's asking you to move the suitcase,' said Ajay.

'But why is he sorry?' Saif shook his head, then addressed the waiter. 'No.'

The waiter looked taken aback.

'No?'

'No,' said Saif firmly. 'If I lose the suitcase, I lose tools that I have carefully collected, polished and kept in mint-fresh condition for years. If I lose my tools, I cannot make astronomical instruments, and if I cannot make astronomical instruments, I will be unable to find the meteorite, and if I am unable to find the meteorite, I will not get a printing press – you see?'

The waiter looked lost. Ajay felt for him. 'Saif, the other side of the carriage will be safe enough.'

'The breakfast cart,' added Vinod tactfully, 'won't be able to get through unless you move the suitcase.'

That decided it. Saif moved the suitcase to where everyone else's luggage was kept, and the waiter brought round the breakfast cart. Ajay's eyes widened. There was enough food on there to last them a month!

Holding a cup of steaming coffee in one hand, and juggling a plate of mangoes, sweet custard apples and jewelled figs, Ajay felt the tension in his shoulders start to ease. After all, the meteorite was just within reach, and his friends were all around him. Yasmin was intently drawing quick charcoal sketches of the carriage in her notepad; Jai and Vinod were quietly swapping stories and strategies to survive on the streets; Saif was busy pouring three different types of sugary cereal into his bowl.

Ajay yawned. He was so tired – too tired even to come up with a headline. The train, with its scent of sandalwood and buttery polish, cream and green cushions, and candle-soft lighting, was very comfortable. Perhaps a little nap? Ajay drained the coffee and finished the fruit and put the empty plate on the table. He felt his eyelids lower, heard the soothing rumbling of the train, felt his eyelids drop, open, close again and his thoughts begin to drift . . .

After what seemed like only a few minutes, Saif's anguished cry shattered the silence, waking him up with a jolt.

'Ajay! The suitcase – it's gone!'

6

Ajay's eyes snapped open. The train had stopped, having reached its final destination. Instead of rosy sunlight outside the windows, there was now darkness, and every glittering light in the carriage had been switched on, their reflections flaring and glaring in the glass.

Saif was standing in front of him, his fists clenched, the panic in his eyes barely held down. Jai was standing protectively near him.

Vinod jumped off the seats, from where he had been looking above the holding area: 'It's not here.'

'Nor here,' said Yasmin from underneath the seats.

And Saif's suitcase wasn't in the luggage area

either. Ajay looked around – all the other passengers were still in the carriage, waiting to get out.

All, that is, except the man in the grey suit.

'Out there!' Ajay cried.

He raced out of the carriage door, off the train, through the ticket barriers, out of the thronging station, into the blast of Jaipur heat. Everywhere he turned there were sellers, passengers, children, hawkers, but he couldn't see the man in the grey suit, or Saif's suitcase, anywhere. Jai, Vinod, Yasmin and Saif, breathless from having run out of the station, joined him.

'He's gone,' said Ajay.

Saif's shoulders slumped. He sniffed.

'But don't worry, brother Saif!' said Ajay, rallying. 'We are the reporters (and editor) of *The Mumbai Sun*. We will find the man in the grey suit, and your suitcase.'

'A man in a grey suit? But why has he taken just Saif's suitcase?' said Jai, puzzled. 'Not the tourists' gold luggage, not money, not jewellery, just . . . oh . . .' He trailed off.

Ajay opened his mouth, then closed it again as realization dawned.

'He is on the hunt for the meteorite too,' said Vinod, for once speaking more words than necessary. 'What better way to slow us down than by taking Saif's metal-working tools?'

They looked at each other in consternation.

'Ajay, we're not in Mumbai any more,' said Vinod at last.

Vinod didn't need to say anything else. Ajay knew what he meant. Mumbai was theirs: they had friends there; they had *The Mumbai Sun*. Here, in a strange city – without his mother's fountain pen, and now without Saif's tools – they were lost.

Ajay squared his shoulders. They were the team behind *The Mumbai Sun*! What was the quote that Niresh had read to them by a writer called Shakespeare?

'Muster your wits; stand in your own defence.'

That was all they had to do! Muster their wits!

He turned to Jai and Yasmin. 'We need friends. Do we have any here?'

Yasmin bit her lip. 'There's a slum nearby. Mrs Jodha, from the T-shirt factory, told me about it. She's travelled to Jaipur in the past looking for work. The kids there are jewellers. They might help us.'

He knew everything would be OK! 'If the kids at the slum work as jewellers they'll have metal-working tools. Saif can use their tools to make the astronomical instruments he needs,' he said excitedly, walking forward.

Yasmin sighed and, grabbing his arm, pulled him back. 'I said "might", Ajay. They *might* also see us as outsiders encroaching on their turf. Mrs Jodha warned us to be careful.'

'Don't worry, Yasmin!' said Ajay. He looked at Saif, whose eyes had flared with hope at the mention of tools. Of course the jewellers would help Saif! He was Ajay's oldest friend. How could they see him and not do everything they could to make him feel better?

Jai's gold eyes flickered as if he was about to say something, but then his mouth tightened as if he thought better of it.

They started on the road. Using her skills as an artist, Mrs Jodha had drawn them a precise inked map of the city, marking the slum's location with a cross. Vinod and Jai went in front and used the map to navigate; the rest of them followed. Ajay looked around in awe. Even at night, Jaipur was rose-tinted and magical – the buildings lit up so that they glowed softly, the colour of sugared petals. On the side was the facade of a five-storey sandstone building jewelled with hundreds of tiny windows and alcoves, with filigree screens and patterned balconies.

'The Hawa Mahal,' said Yasmin softly beside him. 'The Palace of the Winds. It was there so that women confined to purdah could watch what was happening in the city.'

'It's beautiful,' breathed Ajay, getting out his notebook to take notes (for a travel piece about pink buildings for *The* (faluda-pink) *Mumbai Sun*!). A small monkey swung past, grabbed Ajay's notebook out of his hand and leapt on to a wall out of his reach, mocking him.

Ajay ran after it, stopping when he heard Saif's voice calling out. 'Leave the monkey, Ajay! We need to beat The Man in the Grey Suit to the meteorite!'

Ajay waved his fist (at the monkey, not Saif), then ran to catch up with the others, who were weaving amongst hooting scooters and musky, marigold-scented passageways. They passed in single file through narrow streets where tie-dyers on moonlit rooftops unfurled glowing twisted ropes of creamy white fabric dyed with shimmering blue and indigo waves. Yasmin walked as if in a dream, her hand sometimes raised – as if by touching the fabrics, buffeted by the soft breaths of wind, she could absorb the skill with which they were made. Ajay had never seen her so lifted, so utterly entranced.

Finally, they skidded to a stop in front of a labyrinth of small buildings, as Vinod said quietly, 'We're here.'

7

The streets in this part of Jaipur were still lit and thronged with people, but the atmosphere was different – charged – as if it had been laced with gunpowder. There were men and women circling the pathways on scooters, some holding open envelopes filled with semi-precious stones that looked like dull sugar crystals; from the windows came the hissing whine of circular blades; and out of the corner of his eye Ajay could see workers on open patios melting objects with the stop-start flare of blue-green gas flames.

But it wasn't what he *could* see that was causing worry to skitter underneath his skin. It was what he *couldn't*.

It felt as if they were being watched.

'Ajay, I'm not sure about this,' said Vinod gently, crossing his arms – which, for Vinod, was the equivalent of running around screaming.

Ajay was about to agree that if *Vinod* felt scared, Ajay, the (brave, fierce and lion-hearted) editor of *The Mumbai Sun*, would agree (for the good of the team) to listen and (with much reluctance) head back.

But then he saw Saif's face.

'We have to go on,' Ajay said shortly.

Vinod nodded slowly, but Ajay noticed how he was now taking charge of reading the map, leaving Jai and Yasmin to warily watch the moving shadows across the rooftops. Jai's knuckles were white around the handle of the cricket bat.

Ajay looked up too, his eyes snagging on the waxing moon that lay low and heavy in the sky . . . and ran straight into Vinod's back.

'Ow!' Ajay cried, holding his nose as it squashed on impact.

'Dead end,' whispered Vinod, coming to an abrupt stop, his shoulders tense as he stared at the closed-off path in front of them.

There were the sounds of flying thuds and sudden cackles and jeers behind them.

Ajay, Jai, Saif, Vinod and Yasmin whirled around.

They were blocked in.

One of a group of figures, standing in a semi-circle in the shadows, stepped forward into the light – a girl with leaf-green eyes and a missing finger. She smiled at them crookedly, without any trace of humour.

'"Dead meat", you mean,' she said.

8

The two groups faced each other, rigid, each watching and waiting for the other to make the first move.

In the frozen silence, Saif jumped forward and hurriedly pushed Ajay to the front. 'Now is the time, Ajay. Speak to them and tell them that we need help to find metal-working tools and the meteorite.'

Ajay gulped. Fear rippled through him.

There was a tap on his arm. Slowly he turned around to where Saif was looking up at him. 'And Ajay – don't forget we're in a hurry.' Saif gave him a quick, comforting pat on the shoulder and then ran backwards, behind Vinod and Jai and Yasmin.

Ajay turned back. The group of kids of all sizes surrounding them had their arms up, ready to fight. It was now or never! He took a deep breath. 'Friends, Jaipurians, countrymen.' And then, getting into the spirit of things, he continued, 'Lend me your ears!'

Jai wrenched him back just before a pebble whistled past Ajay's own (very delicate) ears.

The girl in front of them looked fierce. 'You're outsiders. Get out of here. Or else.' Her voice sounded like smoky coffee. Her leaf-green eyes glittered.

Ajay shook his head. 'We need your metal-working tools. So we can't leave until you give us them,' he bargained. 'Not to keep!' he added hastily, as the Jaipur kids stepped closer, hostility etched on their faces.

Jai's voice was low. 'We have to get out of here. Now.'

Ajay bit his lip. Jai was hardly ever afraid. But they were outnumbered three to one. What choice did they have?

Then Ajay had a brainwave!

He smiled, relaxed and comfortable now that

he had a foolproof plan. 'This is the Slum-Kid Cricketer,' Ajay said, introducing Jai to everyone.

There was a hushed silence. 'The Slum-Kid Cricketer?' someone whispered in awe. 'Here?'

Jai blinked at the sudden stares in his direction. He stumbled back. 'Ajay, no.'

'The best cricketer in Mumbai?' said the girl. Hope flashed in her eyes and was immediately squashed – but not before Ajay had seen it. 'Prove it,' said the girl, her voice strangely flat as if she was deliberately trying to keep any excitement from bleeding through.

'Go ahead, throw a ball at him,' invited Ajay politely, waving in Jai's general direction.

'Ajay, no,' repeated Jai, his face strained, his gold eyes dark.

'It's OK, Jai. Hit the ball, get a six!' Ajay stepped back, relaxed. Once Jai hit the six, the Jaipur kids would have to believe it was him. Then, star-struck, they would help Ajay and his friends find the meteorite, win the money, get the story and go back to Mumbai as heroes. It was, thought Ajay happily, a very good and completely foolproof plan. He watched a boy from the crowd run forward, a battered cricket ball in his hand. He gave it a top spin that for any other cricketer might be an issue, but for Jai – the best cricketer in Mumbai – would be an easy—

Jai missed.

Ajay jumped.

Jai missed?

Jai never missed.

Ajay rubbed his eyes in shock. Vinod, Yasmin and Saif were rooted to the spot in disbelief.

Jai was still and pale. The cricket bat was still halfway up in the air. In his eyes was trapped and silent agony.

Ajay instinctively reached out his hand, desperate to take away Jai's hurt – but with no idea how to do it.

'Liar,' the green-eyed girl said softly to Ajay,

anger flashing where the hope had once been. 'Get them and show them how we treat outsiders who come inside our city wall.'

Vinod and Yasmin stepped up, so that they stood side by side with Ajay and Jai. The Jaipur kids looked dangerous. This was going to be painful. Ajay closed his eyes.

And then he heard Saif's voice squeak. 'No.'

9

Ajay opened his eyes. Saif pushed through him and Yasmin, and stood in front of them all, a very small figure alone against the gang of kids of all different ages in front of him.

'Saif, get back!' Ajay cried out.

Saif ignored him. Instead he took a further step forward, his hands curled into fists. 'I am Saif. I am an apprentice engineer. I (my friends too, but especially me) need your help to look for a meteorite. I can do it, but I need tools to make the astronomical instruments I need to plot its path. And I must find it because it's the only way that it will come true – my dream. My dream to' – Ajay waited for him to say win the prize money and buy his printing press – 'go to a space station,' Saif proclaimed into the starry air.

Ajay's head spun. He turned to the others, but Yasmin, Jai and Vinod looked equally lost. Since when had Saif cared about space stations? Even Ajay didn't really care about them, except in so far as they made a good news story for *The Mumbai Sun*.

'I am an apprentice engineer,' Saif continued, his stance rigid, his voice stiff as if each word were being said for the first time. 'I want to build things. I've always wanted to build things – big, impossible things . . .' Saif lifted his head. 'I can't even jump more than this.' Saif jumped a bit to demonstrate, creating small puffs of dust beneath his feet. 'But engineers built a rocket that flew and landed all the way there.' He pointed to the moon, which to Ajay now looked distant and alien.

Saif's figure was outlined in silvery moonlight. 'I want to build machines like that – machines that change everything.'

'You want to change the whole world?' said Ajay in surprise. Even with *The Mumbai Sun* he had only thought of changing Mumbai!

Saif turned to Ajay and spoke privately, as if it were just the two of them, and clarified. 'Not just the World. The Universe.' He turned back to the crowd.

Stunned, Ajay faced the crowd too. They stood in silence, as did he, Vinod, Jai and Yasmin, caught by Saif's words, trying to grasp the immensity of what Saif wanted to do.

Then the silence shattered.

'You're a fool,' said the leaf-green-eyed girl, shrugging her shoulders, her voice dripping with ridicule. 'Change the universe? As if a slum kid will ever get the chance! And who are you changing things for anyway? Rich, powerful people who want holidays in space?' Others started jeering Saif around her. She stepped forward and jabbed Saif in the chest. 'Why should we help you with that? Forget about space. Why don't you worry about surviving instead?'

As if at a signal, the older Jaipur kids bristled and moved closer, a threatening light in their eyes. Vinod imperceptibly shifted his stance, Jai tightened the grip on his bat and Yasmin crumbled chalk in her hand, ready to fling at the first person who attacked.

Saif's shoulders slumped. 'You don't under-stand.' His voice was lost, heartbroken. 'I can't forget about space. It's not just there for billion-aires and politicians to dream about. It's there for me. Even if I am just an apprentice engineer.'

Ajay had never heard Saif speak like this. Saif was his oldest friend, and yet he had not under-stood how big Saif's dream was and how important it was to him to win the trip to the space station. The green-eyed girl was right about that, if nothing else – they had to win the prize because how else would Saif, a railway kid, get to work on a rocket?

Ajay's heart dropped. He knew what he had to do, but he could not bring himself to do it.

The line of Jaipur kids came closer, holding up their fists in some cases and sticks in others.

Jai, Vinod and Yasmin crouched.

Ajay felt his stomach lurch. He had no choice. If he couldn't convince the Jaipur kids to help Saif, The Man in the Grey Suit would get to the meteorite first and all would be lost anyway. He took a deep breath and stepped forward. He spoke quietly and directly to the girl. 'You and your friends will help Saif find the meteorite.' The girl started to shake her head, but Ajay stopped her. 'You will help him, because if we find the meteorite we'll give you the prize money. All of it. Every rupee.'

Ajay heard gasps from Vinod, Jai and Yasmin behind him.

The girl's leaf-green eyes went wide.

Ajay pushed back thoughts of his mother's pen. There would be another way to get it back. He would *find* another way to get it back.

Having said what he needed to, Ajay turned to Saif, who looked as shocked as the others, and held out his arm.

Saif hesitated, his eyes filled with trembling hope – the trace of a tear he had blinked away caught in a thread of starlight.

Then he clasped Ajay's arm and smiled back.

10

Ajay was sitting with Yasmin on the floor inside an old warehouse with two rooms split by an open doorway, the door itself swinging off its hinges. The older Jaipur kids were making space on the ground for Ajay and his friends. The younger ones were already curled up and asleep against each other.

'Are you sure about giving away all the prize money to the Jaipur kids?' Yasmin asked quietly. 'What about the printing press?'

Ajay had thought about nothing else since making the promise. He had to get his mother's pen back. But he had a plan! 'It's OK, Yasmin. All we need to do is get to the space station, write the story of the century, find a way to print it (without a printer), and then sell newspapers across India. We'll get all the money we need for the printing press – and more.'

Yasmin opened her mouth as if to say something, then shook her head. Ajay hoped it was in awe. He couldn't bring himself to think about any other possibility.

Next to them, Ajay could hear Saif as he ploughed his way through the rusty metal tools that the Jaipur kids were bringing out for him with infinite patience. 'No. This drill won't do. Nor this soldering iron. I am an apprentice engineer looking for a meteorite – I need metal-working tools in tiptop condition!'

Opposite, Vinod and one of the Jaipur kids, a girl with clipped-up hair, dyed blue, were (both as silent as each other) pouring frothy chai from a kettle into a piece of muslin, twisting and re-twisting the material, to squeeze out the liquid into a metal container on a coal brazier.

The woody, spicy smell of cinnamon bark filled the room.

The girl with leaf-green eyes, Laxmi, brought

two glasses of steaming chai for him and Yasmin.

'What is this place?' Yasmin asked Laxmi.

'Our workshop,' said Laxmi. Then, seeing Yasmin's genuine puzzlement, added defiantly, as if Yasmin had demanded an explanation, 'The money you give us will let us buy proper tools to make it into a workshop. The oldest of us can escape the factory and work here whilst the younger ones go to school.'

'Is where you work now that bad?' asked Ajay.

Laxmi looked at her hand with its missing finger and nodded. There was no expression on her face.

A young girl – only about four years old – whispered from her sleeping mat, 'It feels like the factory's always watching us.'

Hearing her, Laxmi got up and knelt by her, telling the story of the freedom fighter Rani Chennamma until, comforted, the young girl fell asleep.

Then, as if resolving a debate inside herself, Laxmi stood up and brought a small tin box to Yasmin. Yasmin opened it, and with exquisite care took out a shimmering pendant nestled in a scrap of tissue paper.

'Did you make this? It's extraordinary,' whispered Yasmin. The pendant was framed by an intricate web of silver metal, encrusted with stones polished like diamonds and sprinkled with a dusting of mirrors.

Laxmi shrugged. 'It's just glass and tin,' she said carelessly as she took it back, but Ajay could see how deep her pleasure was at their reaction. And in the light, he noticed for the first time a tiny bracelet, like a thread from a spider's web, on Laxmi's wrist. He marvelled at her skill.

'If we have a workshop,' Laxmi continued, 'one day I might be able to design and make a real Kundan pendant from soft gold.'

She turned to Yasmin. 'Show me some of your drawings.' Then, as if the word had been dragged from her, 'Please?'

Yasmin picked up her sketchbook, and the two artists slowly became lost in talking about lines, and shading, and colour. Ajay bit his lip. Friendship didn't seem to care about whether you were from inside or outside a wall. A sheet slipped out of Yasmin's sketchpad and floated down. Ajay picked up the drawing and jumped off the bench in excitement, the chai sloshing in his cup.

'It's him!' he cried. 'The Man in the Grey Suit!'

It was. Yasmin had captured him in soft, blurred charcoal lines: his powerful build, the cut of his jaw, his eyes, the silver tiepin, with the number '4' delicately embossed on it, that slashed diagonally across his tie.

'I drew all the people in the carriage,' Yasmin said, remembering. 'He's the one who stole Saif's metal-working tools,' she added for Laxmi's benefit.

'We need to find him,' said Ajay. This was back to what he knew: being an investigative reporter! He turned to Laxmi. 'Can you get copies of this picture to the other kids in Jaipur? Find out who he is and where he is staying?'

Laxmi stood, put her fingers in her mouth, and whistled. Ten young kids ran up to her. She gave them the picture and a few swift instructions. The kids nodded and ran to a corner with the picture,

Yasmin's box of charcoal and a box of old flyers to trace the picture on the back of each. Soon kids working in and near every expensive hotel in Jaipur would have one.

Ajay could barely keep his excitement from spilling over like the chai he had just dropped. This was more like it. All they needed now was for Saif to find tools with which to build a navigation device for the meteor—

'There are no metal-working tools precise enough!' Saif's cry could be heard across the room, as if he had heard Ajay's thoughts. He puffed as he came over to them. 'It is no use, Ajay. I am an apprentice engineer. I am not a magician. The tools aren't enough to make the astronomical and navigational instruments I need.'

'Astronomical instruments?' said Laxmi.

'Instruments which can be used to navigate using the sun and stars,' explained Saif. 'It is a very difficult thing to do. If we're going to compete with The Man in the Grey Suit to find the meteorite, we need precise, modern instruments with tiptop technology.'

'Precise, modern instruments with tiptop technology,' Laxmi repeated.

Her leaf-green eyes lit up like a tiger's. 'I know where you might find them.'

11

Ajay and Saif looked up.

'Ajay, when I said I needed astronomical instruments, I thought I also said, "precise, modern instruments with tiptop technology",' said Saif.

The stone structures in front of them glowed in the pale dawn light: cylinders, walls, stairs, spheres. Against the sparkling blue sky they looked like vast biscuit-coloured sculptured toys dropped in a giant's playground. Ajay flicked through an Indian guidebook Niresh had given to him about Jaipur and read out the entry. 'The outdoor observatory was built by Maharaja Sawai Jai Singh II, ruler of the kingdom of Jaipur in the early eighteenth century.'

He turned to Saif and said comfortingly, 'They are precise. They are tiptop. They are almost three hundred years old. Two out of three is not bad, Saif!'

Saif faced the Samrat Yantra, the largest sundial in the world, with a triangular wall and stairs that seemed to go up and up into the sky. He squared his shoulders. 'Stay here. Watch out for the others. This will take a few hours.' Then Saif walked away from him and purposefully towards the towering instrument, looking tiny against it.

Ajay watched him go. In the sun's warm butterscotch light, Saif's shadow cut impressively across the ground.

Everyone had a job to do, Ajay thought with satisfaction: Saif was finding the meteorite; and Laxmi, Jai, Vinod and Yasmin were searching for The Man in the Grey Suit. All Ajay had to do was stand in the shade and wait!

Ajay stared at the fantastical instruments in front of him. He imagined the maharaja at the site, before the observatory had been built, looking out at a haze of pink dust and crumbling rock. He and the maharaja would have got on well, he thought – they both dreamt big!

As if drawn in by an invisible string, Ajay slowly walked around the instruments. He took in the huge metal frame of the astrolabe (the largest in the world), the crystalline, sparkling surfaces of two marble-slabbed bowls that mapped the sky (invented by Jai Singh himself) and the jagged pieces of what looked like an enormous Jenga game.

It was as he was staring at an illustration of Leo the lion, on one of the twelve zodiac instruments, with its wavy tail, cute whiskers and mischief-filled eye, that he heard voices to his side and looked up.

'Archaic. Honestly, if it hadn't been for Britain, India would still be an illiterate, non-industrialized backwater,' said a man with a thin, wispy beard to a group he was with.

Ajay's mouth fell open.

'Excuse me,' said Ajay.

The man recoiled. 'We don't have any money.'

Ajay shook his head. 'I don't want your money. I want to tell you that you're wrong.'

'*You* want to tell *me* that *I'm* wrong?' The man laughed, relaxing, amused. 'I am a Professor at one of the most prestigious Universities in the world.'

'And I am a railway kid,' said Ajay, undaunted, 'but even I know that India was not a "non-industrialized backwater" when the British came.'

The tourist laughed. 'Science, with a capital "S", young man, was developed in Europe! It was brought to India.'

Ajay stared at him, stunned. How could he say that? They were standing in Jai Singh's beautiful observatory! One where the stone instruments were created using science from Islam and Hinduism, and where the maharajah had done everything he could to bring together astronomers and books from different lands.

The observatory wasn't just a scientific institution – it was a reminder! A reminder that science was developed by people and countries around the world.

Ajay opened his mouth to argue. In the corner of his eye, he saw Vinod, Jai, Yasmin and Laxmi running towards him.

'Ajay – we've found the hotel where The Man in the Grey Suit is staying!' shouted Vinod, his brown eyes snapping with excitement.

Saif, running down the huge triangular wall, shouted at them. 'Forget everything else! I've tracked the path the meteor took against the skies. I know where it must have fallen. We need to go!'

Ajay looked for a moment at the tourist. The tourist looked back at him with smug superiority. Some (not all) of the other tourists around him looked uncomfortable.

Ajay closed his mouth. He felt sorry for the

tourist, for travelling all this way and still seeing India as he had always done – a former colony and nothing more. The world must seem pretty dull if you constantly saw every other culture as inferior.

Still, Ajay's time was too valuable to argue with someone who would never see him – or his ancestors – as equal. Ajay had work to do.

He turned back to his friends.

'You heard Saif!' said Ajay. 'Let's go!'

The hotel would have to wait.

The race for the meteorite was on!

12

Ajay stood with the others looking in awe at the zigzagging path that ran up the towering Amber Fort. Nothing had prepared him for the sight of the vast sandstone citadel with its powerful walls. It sat on top of the hill, glowing in the sunlight like an eagle spreading out gold-flecked wings.

'How are we going to get to the top?' he said out loud.

'Walk?' said Vinod, crossing his arms and looking as if he was trying to judge the distance.

'I might have another way,' said Laxmi. 'Wait here.'

Ajay squinted up, his eyes burning with the

glowing sun-warmed beauty of the fort. They were all exhausted as it had taken them time to get to the fort in the first place. The half-hour bus ride on the main road from Jaipur's Ajmeri Gate to Amber had been crowded and bumpy. The bus driver, Laxmi's cousin (several times removed), who had let them on for free, had waved back to them, apologizing profusely for their discomfort several times.

'Meet my friend, Sanjay,' said Laxmi, returning with a boy who looked about Jai's age and gave them a wide smile.

Ajay would have smiled back if it weren't for the huge elephant that was thudding along behind Laxmi and Sanjay, and was staring Ajay down with its big intelligent eyes.

'Sanjay is an elephant handler,' said Laxmi – a statement which, in the circumstances, Ajay felt was both unnecessary *and* superfluous. 'Not all the elephants here are well looked after, but Sanjay does look after his well. We can go up in turns.'

And so it was that a while later, Ajay and Jai, the last ones to go up, were sitting up on top of the elephant.

Ajay looked down at the rumbling pathway below and shuddered. He really had nothing against elephants. He *liked* elephants. He liked their wise, crinkled eyes, he liked their grey, leathered hides, he even liked their peanut-searching trunks. What he did not like was sitting on top of one, swaying back and forth, as it lumbered up the winding pathway to the fort. Even with all the cushions, it was sore and dizzying.

What made it worse was that Jai had so far been silent for the entire ride up. In fact, he had been silent ever since he had missed the shot when the Jaipur kid had thrown the cricket ball at him. Ajay knew that the best thing to do when someone didn't want to talk about something was to be tactful and avoid the subject – to give the person time, space and freedom to confide when they were ready.

The second-best thing—

'How did you miss your shot, Jai? You never miss.' He blurted the words out.

Jai's jaw clenched into hard lines and angles.

Then Jai looked at him, his golden eyes lit up like a storm.

Ajay wished he could back away, but there was only limited room on top of an elephant. Instead he fell awkwardly silent and gripped tightly on to his seat.

Altogether it was a relief when they finally reached the top of the hill and the elephant knelt to let them down. Jai leapt off, landing gracefully on his feet. Ajay, trying to copy Jai's elegance, ended up doing a roly-poly as he rolled off. He landed with a thump, sitting down, facing the entrance to the fort.

The others were all there waiting for him.

'Look!' said Laxmi, as she and Yasmin helped him up.

Discomfort forgotten, and waving thank you to Sanjay, who gave him another wide, friendly smile, and the elephant, who waved goodbye with its trunk, Ajay looked up.

Looming over them was the huge entranceway to the Amber Fort.

Suraj Pol.

The Sun Gate.

13

A few hours later, Ajay and Saif were standing on the sandstone wall of the Amber Fort. Saif was looking over it, scoping out the surrounding landscape of the rugged Aravalli Hills, and the dipping valleys, with a little metal telescope. Laxmi and the Jaipur kids had spent the night before making and polishing the telescope, and Laxmi had presented it to him with shy, quiet pride.

'Are you sure the meteorite is here?' Ajay asked.

Saif put the telescope down for a moment and scowled.

Ajay backed away – Saif was very tense at the

moment. They all were, despite the warm syrupy heat.

They had got past the guards and into the vast fort through Suraj Pol (the Sun Gate) – the name had to be a sign of good luck! If the outside of the fort had been imposing, the inside was spectacular.

They had wandered through its multiple court-yards, shimmering gates and the Hall of Mirrors whose walls were covered in a mosaic of glass-work. (Ajay longed to come back at night and light a candle inside the hall, creating a constella-tion of a thousand fiery stars.)

But they had not found the meteorite.

Sunk in a gloom, Saif had sat in the middle of a courtyard in the fort with his head on his fist, deep in thought – looking much like a statue that Ajay had seen in a book about some sculptor called Rodin. Then, with a sudden burst of energy, Saif had scrambled to his feet. 'I've miscal-culated! It's not *inside* the fort – it's *outside*. We need to get to a viewpoint to find it!'

And that's how they'd ended up standing on the wall of the fort looking for the crater of the fallen meteorite.

Ajay glanced at Jai who was standing a little way apart with Vinod, Yasmin and Laxmi, keeping watch for guards asking for tickets. It was as if Jai had built his very own wall around himself. Ajay ached with wanting to ease whatever Jai was going through – but how could he help if Jai wouldn't even speak to him?

'You look! I can't see it!' said Saif in frustration, handing the telescope to Ajay. Ajay took the cool metal cylinder and looked at the landscape beyond the fort – and almost toppled over. Everything was so close! Instinctively, he raised his hand trying to touch the edges of the burnt-orange and green hills, the still, jade-like surface of the Maota Lake, the star-like pattern at the centre of the Saffron Gardens. It was the first time Ajay had looked through a telescope. In the shadowed scrubland in a distant valley, he could even make out a strangely blackened tree that looked like a question mark. He took the telescope away from his eye, marvelling that something so simple – a tube with two pieces of glass – could completely change the way things looked.

'We do not have time to waste,' said Saif crossly, taking back the telescope and putting it to his own eye again.

Ajay, left empty-handed, felt a sudden, sharp sense of loss. He had felt a whole world opening up when he had looked through the lens! No wonder people wanted to go up in a rocket. If just looking through a telescope changed the way you saw things, what must it do to you to see Earth from space?

Saif continued to look at the landscape through the telescope.

'I've got it! I've got it! I've found the meteorite crater!' Saif suddenly cried out in triumph, jumping up and down, his bad mood forgotten. 'The calculations were right! It's just to the east of the road, by the blackened tree that looks like the crane hooks for engines! It was in shade until the sun changed direction and shone on it!'

Ajay felt a jolt of joy course through him. Of course Saif had come through! Of course the team that created *The Mumbai Sun* would find the meteorite!

'Ajay!' he heard Yasmin shout.

Ajay looked at her, and then to where she was pointing.

His blood ran cold. In a group of tourists, just below them, was a man with smoky-blue eyes, watching them, wearing a silver tiepin.

It was The Man in the Grey Suit.

14

The Man in the Grey Suit gave him a long look and turned and sped back out of the fort. He must have heard them shouting out the meteorite's location!

'Let's go!' shouted Ajay.

He and Saif jumped down the stairs, while Vinod, Jai, Laxmi and Yasmin raced from their side of the wall. They met, gasping, just outside the gate, only to see The Man in the Grey Suit get into a sleek silver car with pitch-black windows.

Their elephant winked at them and flapped its ears, ringing a note through its trunk as if blowing a trumpet – but an elephant would be too slow this time. Instead, they ran downhill. Down the pathway, they followed the car, which luckily kept getting blocked by crowds of people coming from the opposite direction. Finally, they reached the spot where the path met the road.

'There he is!' said Yasmin, pointing at the car swerving into the road.

They pushed through the gaps in the crowds on the pavement like pinballs. A rickshaw driver, his parked motorized rickshaw festooned in bright tinsel and red balloons, saw them and smiled.

'I'm Rikesh. Today is my birthday. I can give you a special price—'

'We've got to beat that car!' said Ajay, piling into the back of the rickshaw. Saif fell in next to him, then Yasmin, Vinod and Jai.

Laxmi hung back. 'I'll get the others and follow.'

Ajay nodded, as she ran back into the crowds.

Rikesh, relaxed and happy, began by giving them each a red balloon and draping a piece of feathery tinsel around their necks.

'We're in hurry. It's a race—' started Jai, watching the car with The Man in the Grey Suit drive down the road.

'Time is but a construct,' said Rikesh to him gently. He got into the front and turned the key. There was a throttle, then the engine cut. Ajay felt his heart stop. There was no way that they'd be able to reach the car now. He let out a yelp. Saif was clambering over him, jumping out of the passenger side of the rickshaw and running down to the engine at the front.

Gold sparks flew, screws leapt off and spumes of smoke spiralled. Then Saif, smelling of burning metal and covered in soot, oil and frowns, jumped back in, squashing Ajay into the middle. 'Go!' he commanded.

Rikesh turned the key to the rickshaw.

For a moment – nothing.

Then it roared.

Rikesh looked at them, delight on his face.

'The car?' ventured Jai again, pointing at the silver car that had been blocked by a hooting bus but was now swinging to the side.

Rikesh smiled whilst shaking his head. 'Young people. Always in a hurry,' he said.

He pushed his foot down.

The Rickshaw leapt. Its tyres squealed. It

zoomed forward. Ajay felt himself thrown to the back. Yasmin yelled. Vinod and Jai threw their arms around the others as barriers.

Only Saif seemed unaware of the breathtaking speed – his hair whipping back, his face lined with intensity. 'Go!' he repeated.

The Rickshaw accelerated.

And so did the silver car. It had might and muscle and, as it passed the bus, a clear stretch of road.

Ajay felt his stomach turn. The trees to the side swam and danced; bikes and scooters blurred; dust and grit blasted in front of his face. Ajay gripped on to Saif and Yasmin, as the Rickshaw came edge to edge with the car, getting closer and closer to the silver frame and the dark windows. One of the windows came down and for a moment The Man in the Grey Suit looked past Saif, and straight into Ajay's eyes.

Ajay stared back, chilled to the bone.

The window slowly rolled up.

The silver car swerved, trying to hurtle into them. The Rickshaw tore out of reach, spinning and whirling.

'Keep going!' shouted Saif to Rikesh. And then suddenly added, 'Turn right, over there.'

The Rickshaw flew on, swerved off the road, to the right, and fell forward, rushing through the scrubland.

Ajay screamed, but the wind ripped away his voice.

Everything outside was a blur, a jangle of rocks and scrub and dirt.

Ajay closed his eyes.

The Rickshaw kept moving, tumbling down the valley . . .

. . . screeching to a halt.

And then, what sounded like fireworks popped in his ears.

'Open your eyes, Ajay!' said Vinod, his voice filled with concern. 'We're here.'

Ajay first opened one eye. Then the other. He looked around and saw that the sound of fireworks had just been the balloons popping from the speed! He let out a sigh of relief and allowed Vinod to help him clamber out of the back of the Rickshaw.

They had arrived in an area of vast scrubland at

the foot of one of the cliffs. Ajay could see the trail the rickshaw had made from the road by the dust spiralling up from it in the wind. The silver car was still on the main road, clearly trying to find a safer route down.

He turned around.

Jai, Yasmin and Saif were standing by the blackened tree that looked like a question mark, around a shallow crater in the ground.

Saif had tears of joy running down his face. He turned to Ajay and smiled, pointing down at the dark stone embedded in the crater's centre.

'We've found it, Ajay! We've found the meteorite.'

15

Ajay went to look at the meteorite. Its top, like a rock, was crusted and fused, and its sides were shiny, glossy volcanic black. Where the light touched it, the dark surface shimmered with rainbow colours. If he wrapped his arms around it, his fingertips would only just meet.

Ajay dropped on his knees, feeling the heat of the sun against the back of his neck. Slowly, he stretched out his hand in wonder to where it sat, nestled in the ground like a set jewel. It was cool to the touch. *That was strange*, thought Ajay. After travelling millions of miles he had expected it to still be hot, to still carry traces of its intergalactic journey. How old was it? A billion years old? Older?

He felt dizzy. He touched the strange grooves on the meteorite's iridescent surface. His body tingled. They must have come from its travels through time and space, as it burst past belts of asteroids, blinking stars, whirling planets and glowing moons.

For a moment, he felt what it must be like to be the meteorite – a fragment, separated from home, spinning alone in an empty, dark void.

He shook his head in disbelief. He felt shaken to his core.

'We've won!' he said.

The enormity of the words hit him.

He trembled.

Yasmin, kneeling next to him, shook her head, a soft breeze causing strands of her hair to fly across her face, which she pulled back impatiently. 'We haven't won yet, Ajay. We need to get it to Mrs Surya.'

Ajay's heart sank back into his chest. His one thought had been to find the meteorite! He hadn't thought about how to actually get it to Mrs Surya.

Perhaps special delivery post and packaging?

Would the post office charge extra for objects from space?

Rikesh, busy blowing up more red balloons to replace the ones that had popped, turned to Ajay, his eyes and moustache dancing in excitement. 'This is the birthday to beat all birthdays! You need help to find the billionaire, Mrs Surya? I will get a message to her. I am a rickshaw driver. I have driven everyone, from movie stars to moguls!' He ran to the Rickshaw, turned the ignition and spun the vehicle along the dusty ground in a figure of eight.

Ajay panicked. 'We've got no money to pay you!'

Rikesh waved his hand and shouted over the puttering sound of the Rickshaw's engine. 'Your friend fixed the Rickshaw so that it drives like a Ferrari! That is birthday present enough!'

Then he hit the accelerator, shouted, 'I'll be back!' and drove away, zooming into the distance.

Now they just had to wait.

Saif was staring at the meteorite, his eyes sparkling, his body trembling with awe.

Jai, however, was standing as if his spine were

made of metal. Ajay saw him staring out at the distance, in the direction of the gleaming fort, his hand shadowing his eyes.

In the distance, Ajay could see tiny floating specks. What were they? Crows? Ravens?

'Ajay. Quick. Bring the telescope.' Jai's voice was low, and urgent.

Ajay took the telescope from Saif and went to stand by Jai.

'What is it?'

'I don't know,' Jai said, his gold eyes trained on the horizon like a hawk. He took the telescope from Ajay and looked through it.

His body became tense like a spear.

Ajay snatched the telescope back and put it to his eye. What had Jai seen?

He trained the copper telescope to the place Jai was pointing at. There was nothing to worry about – the burnt-orange and gold ground, the lengthening evening shadows, and—

Ajay almost dropped the telescope in terror.

The Man in the Grey Suit was standing outside the silver car. The car had tried to take a route off track, but was stuck against some straggly shrubs.

Its tyres were churning mud – which must have been the only reason they had been able to get to the meteorite first.

But it didn't matter, because behind The Man in the Grey Suit – rising up like a black menacing cloud of bats from the boot of the car – were about fifteen small, round flying machines with dagger-like claws.

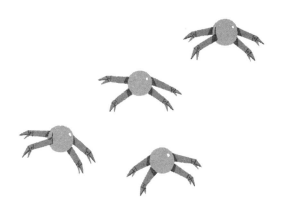

Ajay's heart raced. His chest tightened. He had seen such things on video games being advertised on the television at the station—

He turned to the others. 'Get down!' he cried. 'There's going to be a drone attack!'

16

Saif immediately fell over the crater, covering the meteorite with his body, whimpering, 'The Man in the Grey Suit has taken my tools, he is not going to take this!'

Yasmin and Vinod looked at Jai and Ajay in disbelief. Yasmin snatched the telescope from Ajay and looked through it. 'If you're playing some kind of joke—'

She gasped, her face draining of all colour. Then, handing the telescope back, she grimly took her position in front of Saif. Vinod had already brought out the small, blackened saucepan he always carried in his bag for making tea, to use now as a weapon.

Ajay took a deep breath. 'Jai, if the drones are going to try and grab the meteor, they are going to have to swing low, like cricket balls. You can hit them out of the way – sixes!'

Jai's eyes widened and Ajay could see the whites of them. 'Ajay, no,' Jai breathed. 'You don't understand. I can't.'

Ajay spoke reassuringly. 'Of course you can! You'll be fine—'

'Stop saying that!' Jai cried, agony searing through his voice.

Ajay was shocked into silence.

'It won't be fine! I'll freeze. Just like I did at the match. Ajay, I couldn't help the team!'

Ajay put his hand on Jai's arm to steady him. So that's what had happened? Jai, who had never lost before at cricket, blamed himself for the lost Calcutta match? Ajay knew he had to think clearly. He had to choose the right words and hope that by speaking he would not make everything worse.

In the distance, Ajay saw the black specks in the air were becoming larger. He ignored them.

'Jai,' Ajay spoke softly. 'You tried your best.

Like me being editor! That's what matters!'

'You don't understand.' Jai's voice was full of jagged edges like broken glass, but the words kept flooding out, as if now he had started speaking, he could not stop. 'I keep freezing.'

'Jai.'

'I keep freezing.' Jai was shaking.

Ajay shook his head. Being a friend meant paying attention. And he hadn't because *Jai* was the one that protected *them*. How could he have been feeling like this without Ajay noticing that something was wrong?

'I'm nothing if I can't play cricket,' Jai whispered.

'You are everything,' Ajay said firmly. 'It doesn't matter if you can play cricket or not.'

In the background, Ajay could hear the angry, threatening, mechanical whirring of the drones getting louder and louder. A shrieking wind picked up. Dust swooped in a shadowy swirling vortex around them, pulling and tugging at Ajay's clothes and hair. Ajay ignored them all, keeping his eyes on Jai, his hand still on Jai's arm. 'Don't worry. We're your friends. We have your back!'

'Ajay, I'm scared.' Jai's gold eyes glittered with pain.

'Then be scared,' said Ajay. 'You can be scared around us!'

Jai took a long, drawn-out breath. A shadow fell on them. He and Ajay looked up.

Sweeping towards them were about fifteen drones – black metal balls with claws and wings, like a giant swarm of mechanical flying spiders. They hovered, blotting out the light, whipping up the howling wind and the dust even higher with their choppers.

'Ajay!'

Ajay could hear Saif's voice from behind them as if it were coming from a distance, although he could not be more than a few metres away.

There was no more time.

'We'll be your shelter, Jai,' Ajay said gently. 'For as long as you need.' He was not going to move until he had a sign that Jai was OK – that the terrors no longer had him in their grip.

Jai slowly picked up his cricket bat and looked at it, turning it in his hands.

'What do I do?' His voice was ragged.

Ajay looked at him and felt his heart warm in his chest.

'When you're ready? Take the next shot!'

Jai stared. 'And then?'

Ajay waved at the drones. 'That's all! One shot at a time. We'll take the rest.'

Jai swallowed. He turned, and stood in the correct stance, flicking his bat outwards in the old familiar gesture.

Ajay watched him and breathed again. Then, against the thunderous wind and scraping dust, he stepped next to him to stand with Vinod and Yasmin in a four-person barrier in front of Saif – straws against a swirling tornado.

As one, the drones stopped whirring. A flicker of red and green lights flashed on their bodies.

The battle for the meteorite had begun.

17

The round drones hovered in the air like vultures. Then one, further ahead compared to the rest, flew low and dived towards them.

Next to him, Ajay felt Jai freeze. He reached out, touching Jai's arm. There was no time to do anything more. The drone was hurtling towards them like a small cannonball. As it got closer, it looked bigger and bigger. The dark razor-like claws coming from its round body were slicing through the air, coming towards Ajay's head. He yelped. Next to him, Yasmin flung a stone at it but it just bounced off the metal legs.

'The centre!' shouted Saif from behind them.

'Hit its centre! That's where its AI neural accelerator will be!'

The *what*?

Yasmin flung another stone, and it hit the drone dead centre like a bowling ball.

Stunned, the drone stopped and spun and crashed to the ground.

It blinked out, giving a strange, sharp high-pitched whistle.

'Yeah!' Ajay punched the air.

They'd done it!

The heroes from Mumbai! The team behind the mighty *Mumbai Sun*! The—

'Watch out, Ajay!' screamed Yasmin. Three drones dipped forward and made for them. Ajay dragged Jai, who was still frozen, behind him. Yasmin threw another stone, missed, threw another, pinging the edge of a wing of the one to the left. It jammed, and the drone skittered to the side, its legs in spasms. Vinod stood and yelled as he charged at one with his frying pan. Clang! The edge of a claw got stuck on the bottom of the pan. The third kept coming towards Ajay. He dug his hand into his pocket, pulled out a cricket ball and ran forward, doing an overarm throw and hitting the drone dead in the centre with all the force he had. Bullseye! The drone spiralled and smoked in the air, then dropped lifeless to the ground.

'We're winning!' boasted Ajay, panting.

'Don't be too sure,' said Yasmin, her eyes on the cloud of drones.

Ajay looked too.

He shouldn't have spoken.

The rest – over ten of them – dipped, like cannonballs with deadly claws, arranging themselves in an arrowhead. The red lights on their surface glittered malevolently. Then they attacked – the point of the arrow of drones heading straight for Saif. They were after the meteorite, and no human body was going to stand in their way.

Ajay frantically fished in his pockets for something – anything – to throw at the drones, then turned them out. They were empty.

His breath left his body.

He felt sick.

The drones attacked, churning up dust and wind and flying pieces of metal. Ajay felt the whoosh of them and put his arms in front of his face to protect it. Flying up, the leg of one gashed Ajay's arm. He felt the sharp scissor-cold pain and, fumbling, clamped his hand over the cut that seeped blood.

'Ajay!' Yasmin screamed.

He tried to say something but his jaw had clenched with the pain. Then he looked up.

Cold fear shot through him.

The drones hadn't got low enough!

They flew past in arrow formation. Ajay and Yasmin ducked as the drones whirled up, circling back into position. They beeped furiously, hovering in front of Ajay and his friends, adjusting their dive.

This time they wouldn't miss.

Yasmin stopped frantically tying her scarf around Ajay's arm, and they clutched each other as the drones fanned out behind one another.

Ajay felt a pit of rage in his stomach. What hope did he and his friends have? To the drones, they were just targets, standing in the way of the meteorite they had come to collect with their scraping metal claws.

And then—

'Get down!' Jai shouted from behind them.

There was no uncertainty in his voice. It flowed with command.

'Now!'

Electrified, Ajay, Yasmin and Vinod dived to the ground. Behind them, they heard Jai give a war cry and saw him run forward, a silhouette against the red glow of the sun! He hit out with his bat at the centre of the first drone. Smack! The drone was hurtled away in an arc. And then all Ajay could hear was the sound of wood smashing against metal, again and again. Jai and his bat, in a blur, slamming faster than Ajay could see. Cogs, silver flashing pieces of metal, lights – all spun out in different directions. Having faced down the black hole of fear and doubt, Jai was no longer just the best cricketer that Mumbai had ever seen! He was *more*!

Again and again, he smashed the drones far into the distance.

'Go Jai!' Vinod, Saif and Yasmin cheered.

Ajay punched the air, his fear forgotten. He had his headline!

Boy against machine!

Jai, focused and alert, kept batting. Each shot was seamless and formidable.

And then, all of a sudden, there was nothing. Just empty blue sky – and the wreckage of the drones in front of them like broken metal spiders half-buried in the ground.

Ajay, Vinod and Yasmin stood in awed silence.

Jai turned to them, holding the bat that was smashed into smithereens, looking exhausted but elated. Jai – their friend – his eyes shining with fire and confidence.

'Jai!' Vinod ran towards him, engulfing him in a hug. Yasmin wasn't far behind, knuckling Jai's hair joyously. Ajay flung himself on top of them, throwing his arms around them all and jumping up and down.

Jai had saved them!

18

As they stood, they heard the roaring of rickshaws filled with people with cameras, journalists, members of the public – and the Jaipur kids! Rikesh, the Rickshaw driver, had kept his promise about letting people know they had found the meteorite!

Above them came the thudding sound of choppers. The sound got louder and louder. Ajay looked up, trying to stay standing as the air whipped around him. A helicopter! With breathtaking fluid elegance it landed on the ground in front of them, churning up the earth.

The blades stopped moving, the door of the helicopter lifted open and a tall woman, wearing a sleek jacket, with long, swooshy dark hair and tawny aviator shades, stepped out. The cameras flashed, and there was a roar of spontaneous applause. She walked towards Ajay and his friends looking neither left nor right, as if she hadn't even noticed the other crowds.

She stood in front of Ajay, Vinod, Saif, Jai and Yasmin and took off her shades. Mrs Surya! In person, her eyes were the colour of warm caramel.

'You've found the meteorite?' she said, and she smiled down at Ajay, her smile eclipsing the sun.

Ajay nodded, dazzled by her.

She lifted her head, looking at the meteorite, its surface gleaming in the evening light like a pool of flame. Then she cast a sweeping, imperious glance at the crowds, the cameras and the press. Finally, in a voice loud enough to get picked up by the rolling cameras, she said, 'In that case, I officially declare that the WECU Space Programme competition has been won!'

There was only one response to being attacked by drones, feeling woozy from a gash on your arm, and then finding out you had won the biggest competition in India.

Ajay fainted.

19

He was running, trying to chase down his mother's pen. He could see it! It was hovering just before him! Around him objects were flying – typewriter keys, winged sheets of faluda-pink paper, cricket balls. He swerved.

He had to outrun them!

His mother's pen kept moving further and further away. He had to catch up with it.

Ink blots were moving and spinning on all sides, transforming from blots, to flowers, to twisting serpents.

And then, at the end of the looping, winding, floating road, he saw his mother!

She was standing in front of him, holding her

pen, with star-like flowers in her hair.

'Mother!' he cried. He ran to her.

But as he reached her –

she melted away.

He woke up. And he wasn't in the dream world any more but outside, lying on the ground near the meteorite. A doctor with a beard and a stethoscope was kneeling beside him, looking at him worriedly. Mrs Surya was there too, on the other side. He could only just see her through the unshed tears in his eyes. In the distance he could hear Mrs Surya's bodyguards shouting at everyone, including his friends, to stay back to give him and the doctor space.

'Ajay, it's just a dream.' Against the sounds of the crowd and the bodyguards coming from a distance behind them, Mrs Surya's voice was soft.

He couldn't even nod. He felt so empty inside. It was as if the crowd and his friends were in a different universe – one that he could hear but was not part of. He couldn't even find enough energy to get up.

'The words you were saying . . . I want you to know that I understand what it's like to be alone.'

Mrs Surya's voice, so soft that only he could hear, was filled with a well of regret. She sat back, looking unseeingly at the scene in front of her. Her eyes were dark as she looked into the distance. 'To lose your whole world and have no one to rely on. To have nothing but one object to your name. Our lives are alike in so many ways.' She turned back to Ajay and smiled gently. 'You're safe, Ajay – you just fainted. The doctor's here now – I promise everything will be all right.'

And, soothed by her words, Ajay felt his eyelids close again.

20

Ajay looked at himself in the silver-framed hotel mirror. He was wearing a dark charcoal suit – just like editors wore in all the journalism films! Apart from a bump on the arm, where it bulged over bandages tied by Mrs Surya's private doctor who had helped him recover yesterday, after he had fainted, it was perfect. It had buttons. It had pockets. It had lapels!

Jai laughed, the light in his golden eyes like liquid flames. Ever since the drone attack yesterday, he had been more relaxed than Ajay had ever seen him. 'Enough, Ajay. You look good. So, for that matter, do I.'

Jai did look good. He too was wearing a suit –

his was a dashing white – and in his hands was a brand-new cricket bat, sent to him by Mrs Surya, that smelt of wood and varnish.

'Let's go,' Ajay said, switching off the TV in the room, which had been humming in the background with a documentary about wildlife in Canada. 'We don't want to miss my press conference!' (Mrs Surya had sent a note with the suits that she would delay the press conference until tonight so that he could fully recover.)

They stepped out into the cool marble corridor of one of Jaipur's most expensive hotels. The amethyst evening light fell in through the windows. As they trotted down the corridor, Ajay thought back to the drone attack, which now felt like a strange dream. When he had spoken about the article he wanted to write on the attack to Yasmin, she had shaken her head. 'You can't publish it, Ajay. If you do, no one will believe a word we write again. Not unless there's proof.' She was right. *The Mumbai Sun* needed solid proof that the drone attack had happened *and* that it was linked to The Man in the Grey Suit, if it was going to hold The Man in the Grey Suit to account.

But gathering evidence would have to wait.

Tonight was a celebration!

The hotel was scented with marigolds and amber perfume, and filled with the music of tinkling fountains. As he and Jai walked down the slippery white marble staircase that swept down in a huge arc, Ajay watched the guests walking down in front of them with interest – it wasn't often that he got to observe the rich in their natural habitat! They talked and walked so slowly. It was as if gravity pulled more heavily here than it did in the slums.

Dreamily, he thought again of the fluffiness of the bed in the hotel room and the jets of hot water that streamed out from the taps in the bath. He had never woken up without bruises before. His muscles felt loose and languid. Perhaps, from the outside, he too was walking like a millionaire?

'Ajay!' Ajay and Jai turned to see Saif hurrying down the stairs in a blue serge suit, with Vinod, in his own clothes, beside him, effortlessly taking two steps at a time. Vinod had refused the suit Mrs Surya had sent him, saying he preferred his own clothes. He'd kept his saucepan too.

'Guess my news,' Saif said as soon as he caught them up. And then, too excited to wait, said: 'Mrs Surya's sent me a leather suitcase full of replacement tools! They are not the same as my tools.' There was a momentary pang in his voice, but he shook his head and continued. 'However, they are all brand new, and in tiptop condition.' He lowered his voice to speak confidentially. 'Mrs Surya knows people's worth when she sees them. She sees that I am an apprentice engineer worthy of such an expensive gift.' He waved joyously at some guests who, caught by surprise, waved back.

Mrs Surya's generosity knew no bounds. When she had found out that Ajay could not swim and so could not use the hotel's swimming pool, she had even ordered the hotel to show his favourite journalism films (instead of the ones scheduled) in its cinema!

Ajay was sure that if he asked her to get his mother's pen back for him, she would do that too. The only thing stopping him from asking was his code that journalists had to be independent at all times. He was writing a story about Mrs

Surya's space station.

A suit he could give back; his mother's pen? Never.

But maybe, just this once – just for his mother's pen – he could break his code?

They had reached the bottom of the stairs. The hotel concierge intercepted them.

'Your invitation, sirs?'

Ajay buried the thought of asking for his mother's pen away as far in his mind as it could go, and handed over their invitation from Mrs Surya with a flourish. It was written in dark silver piped so thickly that it rose from the surface on the stiff white cartridge paper. The concierge checked it and handed it back. Ajay carefully put the invitation back into his suit pocket. He would show it to Mr Sandhu, his friend at the stationery stall, when he went back to Mumbai.

As they were led towards two huge intricately carved doors that smelt of sandalwood, Ajay felt excitement flutter in his stomach. He had never been to an event like the one that lay just in front of them. It was just the sort of event where the editor of *The Mumbai Sun* belonged.

The doors opened.

The press conference and dinner were about to begin!

21

Ajay entered the Great Hall of the hotel. His eyes widened. Next to him, Vinod straightened, squaring his shoulders, and Saif muttered under his breath: 'I am an apprentice engineer.'

None of them had ever seen anything like this. The light from a huge crystal chandelier sparkled on to the hundreds of guests. Hexagonal mother of pearl tiles, on the walls and floor, glimmered pale pink and icy blue. Overflowing their vases in fountains of tiny pale stars were white jasmine flowers, their scent perfuming the air. And best of all was the domed ceiling. It was big enough to rival the one at Mumbai railway station!

Ajay was slack-jawed with wonder. The rich

really did live in a different world.

The staff member threaded through the guests, guiding them to their table. Ajay looked around. Where was Yasmin? She had rung Ajay on his very own hotel-room phone (Ajay had never had a phone call of his very own before!) to tell him that she was going down earlier to fill up her sketchbook with drawings before the ceremony began.

He was beginning to get worried when the staff member showed them to a round table with a white cloth, where Yasmin was sitting, busily sketching. She stood up as they came to their seats. 'What do you think?' she asked.

'You look like a queen,' Ajay said at once.

She did! She was wearing her own top and skirt, but now the edges were embroidered with metal work, and mirrors, and tiny seed pearls. 'Mrs Surya gave me all the material and thread I needed,' Yasmin explained, pleased, putting away her sketchbook. 'She said I should be able to wear my own design for the press conference.'

They sat down. Vinod started to look at the menu, his eyes wide with shock. 'I've never heard of half of the things on this.'

'Where are the Jaipur kids?' asked Jai, looking around, his golden eyes taking in the room, as he settled into his chair.

'They'll meet us at the hotel after the press conference,' said Ajay. Vinod looked up from the menu, puzzlement in his eyes. Ajay shifted uncomfortably. He'd asked for the Jaipur kids to be invited, but Mrs Surya had sent an apologetic note that she had to draw a line somewhere. Ajay understood that there might be a limit on numbers but still felt a twinge of guilt at them being left out.

At that moment, two dhol drummers came in, whirling sticks. The thundering beat of their double-sided, barrel-sized drums brought the hundreds of guests to their feet. Ajay stretched to see above them as they raised their golden flutes of bubbly champagne. He couldn't manage it. He jumped on to his chair and then, finally, he saw her!

'Mrs Surya,' he shouted.

She turned and gave a magnetic smile that he was sure was just for him! She looked magnificent as she went to stand on the podium in front of the tables, wearing a silver sari encrusted with scales of diamonds that blazed in the light of the chandelier. Ajay clapped with everyone else until his hands hurt.

'Thank you, everyone,' Mrs Surya said. 'You are incredibly kind. But today is not about me. It is about the winners of the meteorite competition. I therefore call Ajay, Yasmin, Saif, Vinod and Jai – the team behind one of India's greatest investigative newspapers, *The Mumbai Sun* – to come up to receive a cheque for the winning prize money.'

Ajay felt hot as spotlights shone on to their table, cameras snapped, blinding him with their fizzing white light, and people started to clap. So this was what it was like to *be* the news and not just write it! It was like being the sun – the adored centre of the entire solar system! He walked with the others on to the podium, and there was Mrs Surya. Up close, glittering from head to toe, with silver star earrings, and the border of the sari snaking around her, she looked even more striking than from the floor.

'Well done to the team from *The Mumbai Sun*,'

she said, her caramel eyes warm as she gave a cheque to him for more money than he had ever seen in his life.

Ajay held it up in triumph, feeling Yasmin, Vinod, Saif and Jai linking their arms around him.

'For *The Mumbai Sun*!' he said. And then, suddenly remembering, 'And the Jaipur kids!'

The crowd burst into applause.

Mrs Surya nodded. 'But as you know, that is not all. This wonderful team from Mumbai will be staying at my expense at this hotel. Over the next few days they will be covering the lead-up to and the launch of the WECU space rocket to the moon.'

The crowd clapped again.

Ajay would have stayed on stage and given a speech if Mrs Surya had asked but, smiling, she ushered them gently back to their seats. When they had sat down, she turned back to the crowd. 'Let's now hear some words from one of our leading politicians, Mr Jalebi.'

Ajay, back at his table with the others, was so entranced by Mrs Surya that for a moment he didn't notice the tap on his shoulder.

It was only when there was a second tap that he turned around in annoyance, ready to tell whoever it was off for disturbing him.

His annoyance vanished.

'Mr Gupta!' he said joyously.

22

It was Ajay's old friend, Mr Gupta, the managing editor of *The City Paper* in Mumbai, his gnarled face broken into a rare smile.

'Hello, Ajay.' He turned to the others. 'Vinod, Yasmin, Jai, Saif.' The others greeted him with genuine pleasure.

'What are you doing here?' said Ajay excitedly.

Mr Gupta, wearing a name tag with *(he/him)* on it, nodded towards the podium where Mrs Surya was talking to two politicians whilst a third had taken to the stage to drone on about funding for his political campaign. 'I had to be here. It is not often that Mrs Surya speaks in public.'

Ajay looked at her. 'She's wonderful, isn't she?'

Then added proudly, 'Did you hear, Mr Gupta? *The Mumbai Sun* has got exclusive access to the Space Programme!'

Mr Gupta smiled. 'I did. It's a big break.' Then, 'Where's your pen, Ajay? And your notebook?'

Ajay tried to explain. 'A monkey took my notebook.'

'Ahh.' Mr Gupta looked flummoxed. He dug into his jacket pockets. 'No journalist should be without a notebook and pen. Use these until you get your own back. The notebook has a few jottings – nothing confidential.'

Ajay took them and looked up at Mr Gupta with grateful thanks.

There was an echoey tapping on the microphone as Mrs Surya took the stage again.

Mr Gupta made to leave. 'I must return to my table. I'll see you back in Mumbai.' He hesitated, then added, 'This is not our world, Ajay. As journalists we get to swim in it sometimes, but we do not belong – don't forget that.' Then, shaking his head, as if he felt he had said too much, he said, 'Goodbye' and then, 'Good luck,' and was gone.

Ajay waved, licked the ballpoint pen nib and

opened the spiralled reporter's notebook to a clean page, feeling the old thrill at reporting in his fingers!

Mrs Surya was standing still. She waited until there was a hushed silence, then spoke. 'The meteorite has been sent to the Geological Survey of India for testing. But the meteorite's true value is not in its substance but in its message. And its message is this: It is time to cut our ties with Earth! It is space, with its infinite treasures, that holds our future.'

She opened up her arms expansively. Drawn in by her words like a moth to a sparking flame, Ajay leant forward.

'Space offers us new worlds to conquer, new territories to colonize and endless resources to take. Its treasures,' Mrs Surya continued, 'are finally within our grasp.'

Ajay was spellbound. He could see the future! One day, he would travel to distant planets to bring them news from Mumbai! He wrote down what she was saying word for word. He wanted to read the words back to himself when he was alone and could think about them.

Mrs Surya continued speaking, her voice hypnotizing. 'When the Indian Space Research Organization lost its monopoly over Indian space travel, politicians gave me licence to launch a manned rocket to the moon if I agreed to certain restrictions. I also had to agree to their choice of scientist, who has the power to veto projects, to oversee the work.

'There should be *no restrictions*. Entrepreneurs like me, all over the world, have unique capabilities. If allowed complete freedom, we could use our networks and the billions we have made from factories, warehouses and businesses spanning the globe to push the frontiers of science further than they have ever gone before.'

There was a rustling sound in the audience. Ajay looked up in surprise from the notes he was scribbling. It was the first time all evening that people seemed unsure about whether they should agree with her.

Perhaps sensing this, Mrs Surya smiled graciously. 'However, for now, I accept the conditions placed on the Programme. On the fifteenth of March we will be celebrating the launch of the greatest space mission India has ever seen! So please – enjoy your meal, enjoy the evening and know that a new dawn for India and all of humanity is about to begin!'

Reassured, the crowd roared its approval.

Ajay felt his head spin. So many questions! So many ideas!

He rubbed his hands together with joy.

This was the story of the century, and he and *The Mumbai Sun* were right in the middle of it!

23

It was dawn at the airfield just outside Jaipur. The sun was half visible on the horizon, like a wedge of lemon. Ajay yawned. It had been a long night.

After Mrs Surya's press conference and dinner had ended, Laxmi and the elder Jaipur kids had met him at the hotel reception and Ajay had given Laxmi the cheque.

Even now he could feel the trace of the damp fold of paper on his fingertips.

Ajay shook his head. What was the point in wishing that he could have held on to all that money for just a bit longer? He had to focus on what was happening now.

'Here, Ajay,' Vinod said, interrupting his thoughts, as they stood outside waiting for the aeroplane that would take them to the space centre. He passed Ajay a cup of hot coffee from his flask. 'From the hotel.'

Ajay took the steaming hot liquid gratefully and gulped it down. The coffee was oil black, scorchingly hot and bitter. But it woke him up!

Yasmin was looking up into the distance. A small silver plane, that in the air seemed to be no bigger than his fingernail, was beginning its descent.

'It's beautiful,' she murmured.

It was.

The sun's light burnt bright on its metallic wings. It looked as much a part of the sky as a silver bird. Circling closer, causing a gust of wind to blow towards them, it finally hit the landing strip in front of them, lifting up, drifting down again and finally coming to a halt. The whir of propellers slackened. When they stopped, the door was thrown open and the pilot, with vivid features and laughing eyes, jumped out to stand in front of them. 'I'm Anita. My pronouns are she/her. I'll be your pilot for the day. Get in.' Her dark hair was tied in a loose bun, and a turquoise scarf spilt out from the top of the sharp lines of her leather flight jacket.

'Why did she tell us her pronouns?' Ajay asked Yasmin as they got in. He'd meant to ask Mr Gupta earlier why he always wrote *(he/him)* next to his name on editorials and why one of the journalists on *The City Paper* wrote *(they/them)* next to their name.

'Everyone should be safe with sharing their gender and pronouns if they want to,' said Yasmin thoughtfully. 'We need to listen to people when they share who they are and stop dictating or assuming.'

That's what he would do from now on!

The aeroplane only just fit the six of them. Ajay snapped the buckles on his seat belt around his waist and looked out of the window. The bubbling excitement suddenly turned to nerves. He had never been on a plane before. This one, with its splendid wings, was very beautiful but it also looked very *thin,* and now that they were sitting inside, balanced by its legs and wheels, it also felt wobbly. How was it going to carry them up?

'Do not worry, everyone,' Saif said, relaxed and cheerful. 'Planes are just a matter of aerodynamics and engine velocity. Engineers have designed them with maximum safety in mind.'

Vinod did not look comforted. His face was drawn; his hands were clenched at his sides. Jai was no better. Perhaps worse. He was biting his lip, drumming his fingers against the armrests.

Ajay turned to Yasmin. She would say something to drown out the nerves! But she was sitting completely still, focused on the window next to her. Was she OK? Suddenly Ajay realized – Yasmin wasn't frightened. She was fascinated! Just like she was when she was drawing. He hadn't even known that other things could make her feel this way.

He felt a shot of loneliness. It was as if, on the plane, she had no idea that he existed.

Anita, after doing a safety check, had entered the cockpit. She twisted around for a second, handing them some boiled sweets with a smile. 'For takeoff and landing – to help with your ears popping.'

Ears popping?

Why exactly had no one ever mentioned this risk to Ajay? Preferably before he was strapped into the plane and unable to get off.

Before he could ask for details about popping ears, Anita had put on her headphones, checked the dials and flicked some switches. She still looked relaxed, but now was completely focused and alert. Lights on the dashboard turned on and the plane started to thrum – as if it had been asleep and was now being coaxed back to life under her fingers. The plane stirred and began to roll forward, slowly gathering force – and speed!

As it went faster and faster, Ajay's hair swept back. His stomach felt like he'd left it all the way at the start of the runway.

And then the plane started to lift off the ground!

Ajay was thrown back into his seat. As the plane flew up, his ears felt blocked. Pressure was gathering inside. Ajay threw the sweets into his mouth. They were mango-flavoured, and as he rolled them around in his mouth, and crunched, the pressure in his ears eased.

Ajay felt a whoosh!

The plane zoomed into the sky, tearing into the blue and gold.

Ajay closed his eyes, offering prayers to anyone who was listening.

And then, hurtling forward through the atmosphere, the plane began to right itself.

And all at once everything felt still!

Ajay opened his eyes. Through the window he could see the right wing tip of the plane curve towards the path of the sun. It was edged with gold.

He gasped.

And checked himself over.

'Everyone OK?' Anita called from the front.

Ajay looked up. He was still in one piece! Vinod was discreetly being sick in a tiny paper bag, with Jai's hand on his shoulder. Saif's eyes were covered by his hands. Yasmin looked as if her heart was in her eyes.

'I think so,' Ajay shouted back.

The team from *The Mumbai Sun* were a little worse for wear on their first flight anywhere, but they were intact!

24

Ajay looked out of the window from the plane.

He had never seen anything like this! He could see the tops of hillsides and flashes of lakes like splinters of glass. He could see the dusty pink of the city of Jaipur, no bigger than a postage stamp, and the Amber Fort glinting below like a single gold bead. He waved, wondering if the elephant at the fort might sense him passing above and raise its trunk back.

Since leaving Mumbai he had felt homesick. He had felt like an outsider. But he wasn't! You couldn't see city walls from this high up – the land was all just one huge glittering mosaic.

He understood why Saif was obsessed by space now. If Ajay felt lightheaded now, what would it feel like to see the view from a rocket?

His troubles would vanish!

'Isn't it wonderful, Ajay?' Yasmin whispered.

He turned and nodded, the feeling of loneliness gone.

'Are we there yet?' blubbered Saif from behind his hands.

'I think there's still a while to go, Saif,' comforted Ajay.

Eventually, the plane landed, hitting the runway with enough impact that Ajay felt it in his fingertips *and* his toes.

They stumbled out of the plane and it felt to Ajay that, for the first time in his life, he had lost his sense of time. Saif collapsed on the ground. Jai, his eyes flickering gold in the still morning light, held up Vinod, who was looking a bit groggy. Yasmin looked heartbroken that the flight had ended.

Ajay turned and looked at the glass and metal building in front of them, with a giant open eye above a horizontal dagger, the insignia of WECU, etched into the sign at the front.

'Welcome to WECU Space Centre,' Anita said.

25

The space centre towered above them. It was made of opaque glass and steel-grey metal, and looked vast – like a city, not a building. Ajay had never seen anything like it. He pinched himself.

Anita pressed her hand against a panel to the side of the doors. The panel flickered and beeped, and a green light scanned over her eyes. Slowly, the glass doors, which stretched to the sky, slid open. Ajay and the others followed Anita inside – Jai and Vinod visibly nervous and Yasmin looking star-struck. Ajay gripped on to his notebook and pen. Saif was trembling.

'It's OK, Saif bhaiya. Don't be nervous.'

'I'm not nervous,' said Saif, who had now

recovered from the flight and was looking as if any second he was going to burst the seams of his jacket. 'I am an apprentice engineer. This is the greatest moment of my life!' Ajay could see that Saif looked as if he had been hit by a lightning bolt – his eyes and face were glowing with light.

As they went into the blue-black glass building, Ajay felt he could hear a fanfare of golden trumpets ringing in his ears. In front of him was a cavernous space. Suspended from the ceiling, so that it floated in the air, was a machine covered in solar panels, the size of a railway engine. Shaped like a squashed diamond, it twinkled like a giant disco ball! Anita smiled at their gasps, as they bent their necks back to look at it. 'Gets me every time,' she murmured, looking up. 'A replica of Aryabhata: India's first satellite.'

'Vikram Sarabhai is my hero,' said Saif, waving his arm at the satellite with pride, as if he had known Sarabhai personally. 'Creator of the Indian Space Research Organization! It was his work that led to the launch of Aryabhata in 1975!'

Ajay's mouth was open.

Talk of dreaming big!

Anita laughed. 'Come on – this is just the start.'

They followed her around the circular walk-way. Ajay felt very small – like a piece of plankton swimming in an ocean.

They went through a small door to the side and into another room, the largest that Ajay had ever seen. There were people, looking like ants, on giant ladders – clambering over and working on heavy metal engines the size of long-haul lorries. Other people were sitting at computers, and others still were in lab coats working on outer metal casings. Yasmin had already opened her sketchpad. Jai and Vinod were standing together in awe. Saif's arms were open, as if he could encompass the whole scene in front of him in a big hug.

Ajay got out Mr Gupta's notebook, turning it to a new page, and licked the tip of the ballpoint pen to get it working again. His cheeks were flushed with excitement. This was it – the WECU Space Centre – his story for *The Mumbai Sun*!

26

Ajay couldn't be happier. Saif had been speaking with one of the engineers; Yasmin had been finishing off her sketches; Vinod and Jai had been asking Anita questions – all whilst Ajay had stood a little distance away, furiously filling pages and pages of his notebook. He looked up from it now, biting the end of the pen, staring at a silver metal engine and trying to think of a good adjective to describe it. *Colossal? Ginormous? Stupendous!*

Wearing the name tag 'Mrs Kajal (she/her)', a woman who looked like she was in her forties, with hair like a dark cloud and soft brown eyes, had come up to stand next to him. She was wearing a blue and silver chiffon sari that rippled around her like water.

'It's impressive, isn't it?'

'Yes,' Ajay said, smiling at her then looking back for a moment at the engine, unable to take in that soon it would be powering the rocket into space. From nowhere, the memory of the tourist at Jai Singh's observatory and his smug manner came back to him. *If it hadn't been for Britain, India would still be an illiterate, non-industrialized backwater.*

How did racist statements have that power? To burrow themselves inside you, just to dart you with their poisonous memory when you least expected it?

'Are you OK?' Mrs Kajal looked at him, concerned. Ajay realized he was clenching his pen so hard that it looked like it might snap.

'It was something I heard a tourist say that made me angry,' explained Ajay. 'That Science was developed in Europe.'

Mrs Kajal was quiet. It was a lot like being around Vinod. He could see her thinking deeply before she spoke. After a few moments, she nodded, taking it seriously. 'Let me show you something.'

She took him over to a wall. On it were portraits. 'So often we hear that modern science began in Europe and is therefore rooted in the West. But all countries and cultures played their part. Look at these pictures.' She pointed to the wall. 'Jagadish Chandra Bose. A.P.J. Abdul Kalam. Asima Chatterjee. Three names just from India that should be better known.'

'So you don't think colonialism helped India to modernize and stopped it from being an "illiterate backwater"?' Ajay asked, curious.

Mrs Kajal laughed. 'The British left India with only sixteen per cent of people able to read and write, so it definitely *wasn't* colonialism that helped India modernize. The horrors of colonialism were justified by the lie that some races and cultures are superior to others. There are people who continue to promote that lie, trying to silence those who call for equality. In many countries scientists still suffer from racism as a result.'

Scientists?

Ajay did a double take. 'Who are you?'

Anita, who had come over and heard Ajay's question, leant against the wall, her turquoise scarf fluttering around her neck. She answered with dancing eyes. 'Mrs Kajal, *Chief* Scientist at WECU, and the person appointed by the government to oversee its Space Programme.'

Ajay blushed. How had he just assumed from her gentle manner that Mrs Kajal was an assistant?

He opened his mouth to apologize, when Saif's voice cut in, calling, 'Ajay! Look what Mrs Surya's sent us.'

They all turned as Saif ran up to them excitedly, holding a little box. He flicked a switch on its side and a hologram projected up from his cupped hands, flooding the space in front of them. It reflected over their upturned faces and in their eyes: a sparkling mesh of white light that spun slowly, showing 3D images of settlement areas, mining machines and satellite systems.

Mesmerized, Ajay lifted his hand to touch the image. His hand went through it, scattering particles of light like stars.

Mrs Kajal nodded, all expression wiped from her face. 'The plans for the colonies that Mrs Surya wishes to set up on Mars.'

Vinod, who had come over with Jai, frowned. 'Colonies? For who?'

Mrs Kajal hesitated.

Saif was bubbling over with enthusiasm. 'I knew it! I knew it would be possible one day. I'll go! No one in Mars will tell me I am just a railway kid! When I live there, I'll be Chief Engineer – and rich!'

'Won't you miss Earth?' said Vinod, astonished. 'The plants? The food? Us?'

'Who cares about Earth?' Saif shrugged as he switched off the hologram. 'We'd have a new home. You could all come too,' he pointed out generously.

Ajay remembered how beautiful the world had looked from the plane: its emerald, gold and sapphire colours blazing in the sun's light.

'Ajay, you would come, wouldn't you?' Saif insisted.

Ajay hesitated, testing out the calling card in his head: Ajay – Editor of *The Mars Sun*!

He turned to Mrs Kajal with more questions about the settlements, but they died on his lips. She looked haunted.

'Mrs Kajal?'

She opened her mouth as if to say something—

Suddenly, the glass walls around them went dark. Then they flickered and Mrs Surya's face appeared on all four of them, six metres tall. Her caramel eyes looked up and down. She spotted Ajay and smiled.

'Come and see me.'

That was all. Her face disappeared. The four walls went dark again, then changed back to glass.

There was an audible sigh all around. People who had frozen when her image came up on screen bent their heads and hurried back to work again.

Ajay turned his notebook to a fresh page. This would be the interview of the century!

27

The lift to Mrs Surya's office zoomed up like a jet. When they got to the top and spilt out in relief, Anita took them across the shiny glass floor to a door with 'Mrs Surya' written on it. She pressed her hand against the side, and through an intercom said, 'Mrs Surya. We're here.'

'Ajay and Saif only, please,' Mrs Surya's voice said pleasantly. 'The rest can wait with you outside.'

Ajay looked at the others in shock. *The Mumbai Sun* was a team. How could he ask Vinod, Jai and Yasmin to stay away?

Jai shrugged, yawning as he collapsed into a chair outside. 'I'm happy to rest.'

Yasmin turned to Anita. 'Tell me about flying whilst we wait? Please?'

Ajay swallowed. Why was she so interested in flying all of a sudden? Yasmin was the illustrator for *The Mumbai Sun*!

Ajay turned to Vinod, waiting for him to say that he too would wait outside.

Vinod crossed his arms. 'I'm coming in with you,' he said quietly.

There was a moment's silence.

Saif piped up. 'You can't. Mrs Surya said it was just Ajay and me, and—'

'I'm part of *The Mumbai Sun*,' Vinod said. 'I'm coming.'

There was a moment's pause. Jai sprang up and stood beside Vinod, his eyes battle-gold. Yasmin, her body tense, stood on the other side like a shield.

Ajay felt paralysed. What should he do? He was terrified of Mrs Surya turning them away and losing all chance of getting the story and his mother's pen back. Yet how could he leave Vinod behind?

He turned to Vinod. Vinod was staring back at

him, hurt and pain like a flame in his eyes. *Vinod had seen him hesitate to include him.*

Oblivious to what was happening, Saif shook his head at Vinod. 'You don't even care about space. If Mrs Surya says we can't have the meeting because she doesn't want you there, we'll all lose our chance—'

'Enough, Saif!' Ajay exploded. 'Vinod's coming.' He saw Jai and Yasmin breathe a sigh of relief. But even as he said the words, he knew that it was too late. *Vinod had seen him hesitate.*

The door to Mrs Surya's office slid open.

Throwing his hands up in frustration, Saif stalked inside. Defiantly, Vinod followed him. Taking a deep breath and gripping on to Mr Gupta's pen and notebook, Ajay followed Saif and Vinod into the office.

The door snapped shut behind them.

28

Mrs Surya's office was huge! The size of the hotel's swimming pool. It was all glass – including the floor, which showed a drop of a gazillion floors down to the ground. Saif looked down and caught blindly at Vinod to steady himself.

Mrs Surya had her back to them, her hair coiled over one shoulder, and was sprinkling fish food into the tank that lined one of the walls. With twisting coral rising from its depths, the tank was filled with neon-blue fish that swam in one direction then rapidly in another like a razor-sharp arrow. Ajay shuddered. For some reason he had never liked fish tanks. No matter how big they were, they weren't the ocean.

Mrs Surya turned and smiled, and Ajay forgot all about fish tanks. He got his notebook ready. This was the exclusive that would save *The Mumbai Sun* and get his mother's pen back! He would make it up to Vinod later, Ajay promised himself. They were friends! Vinod would understand why Ajay had not backed him straight away once he explained it to him.

'I'm so glad that you're here . . .' Mrs Surya began. Her hooded

eyes flickered. 'I'm sorry,' she said pleasantly. 'I thought I had invited just Ajay and Saif?'

Ajay opened his mouth. Saif, still blindly clutching on to Vinod's arm and clearly terrified of the glass floor, beat him to the punch, bursting out, 'Vinod's staying!'

After a moment, Mrs Surya smiled. 'Of course. My apologies, Vinod – I did not mean to prevent you from attending. I just did not want to bore you.'

Ajay felt a wave of relief wash over him. It was all sorted! Vinod got to stay, and they got their interview for *The Mumbai Sun*! He looked at Vinod to share the relief, but Vinod was avoiding his gaze. Ajay bit his lip. *Later*, he promised himself. He would explain why he had hesitated to Vinod later.

Mrs Surya pressed a control on her desk. The glass floor turned black, looking as if it was solid.

'Saif, it's OK. You can look down now,' Mrs Surya said, her voice kind.

Saif opened one eye, then another, gingerly hopping on one foot and then another. Finally satisfied that the floor would not break underneath him, he let go of Vinod's arm, gave a huge sigh of relief and collapsed on the black steel sofa next to them, helping himself to a glass of fizzy bottled water which he quickly gulped down.

Mrs Surya took a seat and gestured to Ajay and Vinod to take seats on the sofa too. Ajay sat down hurriedly, licking his pen nib. Vinod sat down on the edge, frowning.

Mrs Surya turned her dazzling smile on Ajay. 'What do you think of the space centre?'

Ajay couldn't help but smile in return. It was nice to be asked for his opinions! He always had so many!

'It's out of this world!' Ajay said sincerely.

'Isn't it?' Mrs Surya said. 'It is the culmination of decades of work.' She leant forward. 'Let me tell you a secret, Ajay.'

Ajay, flattered, leant in. After all, one of the most important people in India was choosing him to confide in!

'People in India think that the WECU Programme is just about sending a rocket to the moon, and then to Mars – but the reality is that it is about much, much more.' She looked Ajay in the eye. 'The truth, Ajay, is that we are in a battle over who controls space. Whoever controls space will control Earth as well. Countries around the world have shown that they are capable of smashing down each other's satellites with missiles and of hacking into satellites from Earth. Imagine, Ajay! A single cyberattack on our satellites could destroy our financial system, our hospitals and our aircraft. The Indian government needs the resources of billionaires like me to match the space capabilities of other countries. It needs to be *grateful* to people like me – not impose restrictions on my vision for space – if it wants to stay safe.'

Ajay's voice stuck in his throat. What kind of a future was Mrs Surya describing? Then he realized – it wasn't the future. It was happening now!

'What can we do?' Saif whimpered from behind a cushion. 'All is lost!'

Mrs Surya shook her head. 'No, it isn't, Saif – not at all. Within moments of crisis are great opportunities. Yes, there is a race to control space – but if we win, we will become rich beyond our wildest dreams.'

The diamond ring on her finger glittered like a

star. 'Under international law, countries and people cannot *own* the moon or other celestial bodies, but they can *mine* them. And once resources such as minerals and metals are extracted from space, they can be *sold*.'

Ajay suddenly imagined a giant forklift truck in space, taking large bites out of the moon. If everyone wanted a share, would any of the moon be left to shine at night?

'What about the plans for settlements?' said Vinod sharply. 'What are those for?'

Ajay started. He had been so entranced by Mrs Surya's words that he had forgotten about the settlements.

Mrs Surya looked at Vinod and her eyes filled with delight. 'That is the best part. We don't just get to defend society as it already exists – we get to create a new one! As it is, there are certain politicians around the world who are working towards creating cities or zones in their countries where entrepreneurs will be directly in charge of laws and society! Take that idea to space – and the possibilities are endless.'

She stood up, as if unable to keep still in her

excitement. The sun caught on her diamond earrings and ring, encircling her with blazing light. 'It is my vision for the future. If given free reign, I will be able to create a new society in space – one free from the laws that restrict us on Earth. I will not just mine the moon. I will move factories into space so that they no longer pollute our world. I will save our future!' She whirled, and her face that had been so joyous was suddenly filled with fear. Ajay wanted to comfort her.

'But Ajay, I have not called you here to describe my vision. I have called you here because I need your help!' She stopped, and when she spoke again her voice was full of fear. 'You see, someone is trying to sabotage the Space Programme!'

29

Sabotage! The word reverberated around the room. *How could anyone sabotage the Space Programme?* thought Ajay. *It would destroy the dreams of railway and slum kids across India!* Ajay had seen charcoal rockets scrawled on paper lanterns and rocket graffiti sprayed on to the walls of the station. They were signs of hope. If humans could invent magical and mind-bending machines like rockets, they could definitely solve human-made problems like people not having enough money to live!

Saif popped out from behind his cushion, a frown on his face. He threw the cushion to the side, jumped off the sofa on to the ground and lifted his hands into fists. 'Who is trying to destroy the Space Programme? I'll stop them!'

Mrs Surya looked very fragile. Her eyes were wet, and her smile was sad. 'If only I knew. At first, I thought the saboteur was a competitor trying to destroy our capabilities in space. But now I know it is much worse – the saboteur is someone working on the inside.'

Ajay drew a long breath. Treachery?

If it was someone on the inside, uncovering their identity would require a delicate touch.

Subtlety.

Finesse!

Ajay almost fell off his seat. Of course Mrs Surya had asked for his help! This was a job made for him!

He squared his shoulders, blew on his fingers, licked his pen and turned to a fresh page in Mr Gupta's notebook. He was ready to report!

'Evidence?' he began, in his formal interviewing voice (much deeper than his usual voice).

Mrs Surya suddenly looked frail as she gave him a note.

'Well?' said Saif impatiently. 'What does the note say?'

Ajay coughed. Then, solemnly, read it out. 'Beware the fifteenth of March!'

'It's a warning,' Mrs Surya began to explain. 'It's the date of the launch.'

'It could be a hoax,' Ajay said. Journalists should be sceptical and test evidence at all times!

Mrs Surya shook her head, passing him a map with three crosses on it – one in the area of the space centre marked 'food laboratory', another at the training facility for astronauts and the third in the engineering room. 'We found this in the food laboratory where the first sabotage attempt took place.'

'It fell from the saboteur's pocket?' Ajay asked. What luck!

Mrs Surya nodded. 'It's how we know it is an inside job, and why I need *The Mumbai Sun* on the case. You have a reputation for honesty. You have shown India that you can be trusted. No matter what it takes, I know that you will search until you find the truth. You see, the first sabotage attempt failed,' said Mrs Surya. 'But there are still two crosses left. One at the training facility. The other—'

'In the engine room!' Saif burst out, looking at the map. He pushed his sleeves up. 'Never fear, Mrs Surya! If anything is wrong there, I will find it. I will not let the saboteur succeed. After all, I am the best apprentice engineer in Mumbai – and probably Jaipur too!' he added for good measure.

A single tear of gratitude ran down Mrs Surya's face as she murmured, 'I will give you all top-level security clearance. You will have everything you need to find the person behind this.'

Saif saw the tear and blushed.

Vinod's eyes were still guarded.

Ajay flipped back his notebook, his heart racing. The race for *The Mumbai Sun* to stop the saboteur, before the rocket launch could be wrecked, was on!

30

Full of excitement, Ajay ran out of Mrs Surya's office and stopped short, causing Saif and Vinod to crash into him. Jai was there – snoozing happily on the sofa. But Ajay couldn't see Yasmin!

'Jai!' Ajay cried, shaking him awake (never an easy task).

Jai woke up, his hair falling into his sleepy golden eyes.

'Yasmin. Where has she vanished to?' Ajay said, trying to keep the panic from his voice. What if the saboteur had got her?

Jai yawned. 'Thin air,' he said cryptically.

'This is no time for jokes, brother Jai,' said Ajay firmly.

Jai gave him a sardonic glance and led them through the security doors up and up and up some metal stairs, and pushed open the door to the roof. Ajay gasped at the sudden brightness of the light and the rush of wind swirling at them from all sides. They were even higher than they had been in Mrs Surya's office!

Ajay saw Yasmin at the far end of the roof. Her dark hair swirling, she was standing side by side with Anita looking out in the direction of the airfield. Snatches of Anita's words were carried towards him on the wind.

'. . . always trust your attitude indicator . . .'

From where he stood, Anita and Yasmin looked like sisters: Anita excitedly translating how to navigate the clouds, the sunlight and the infinite blue of the sky, and pointing at the horizon with quick, graceful movements; Yasmin biting her lip in utter concentration to absorb it all.

As Jai, Vinod and Saif cautiously held on to each other, and inched their way to the nearest edge for the view, Ajay went up to Anita and Yasmin, feeling the sweep of wind tug on his hair.

'We should go now, Yasmin,' he said, pulling

slightly on her arm. 'I need to tell you about the meeting with Mrs Surya.'

Yasmin looked at him in surprise, her pencil hovering over the flapping pages of her sketchbook where she had been taking notes. It was as if, just for a moment, lost in the dream of flying, she had forgotten who he was. 'Ajay – is the meeting over?'

Ajay nodded in confusion. Had she not noticed the time?

'I'll just be a few minutes,' Yasmin said, turning to Anita to ask rushed questions about alien things called airspeed, heading and vertical speed indicators.

Ajay waited for her to turn to him again – and, when she didn't, suddenly felt lost.

He heard the door behind him open and the sound of footsteps, and turned to see Mrs Kajal in her chiffon blue and silver sari, coming to stand next to him on the roof. For a little while, they just stood there together quietly.

'Do you like flying too?' Ajay asked eventually, trying to distract himself from the sore feeling unfurling in his chest.

Mrs Kajal smiled, the corners of her eyes crinkling as the wind played with the folds of her blue sari, making them ripple like water. 'No – I leave that to people like Anita and your friend. But this is a good place to be when you need to clear your head.' She massaged her shoulder, and Ajay could see that underneath the smile she looked tired and filled with tension.

'Aren't you excited about the launch?' he asked.

She bit her lip. A frown creased her forehead. 'I will be. But not yet. It could all still go wrong.'

Ajay had never met anyone like Mrs Kajal before. Someone so powerful who admitted to being so nervous. Shouldn't the person overseeing the Space Programme be more confident?

Mrs Kajal spoke softly, as if to herself. 'What if I've made a mistake?'

He was about to ask her what she meant, when he heard Yasmin calling him.

'Ajay! I'm ready now!'

She was running up to him, her eyes and cheeks bright. 'You'll never guess! Anita said I can sit in the co-pilot's seat on the plane ride home so that I can watch the controls!'

Ajay, determinedly ignoring the ache in his chest, smiled happily for her.

Saif, Vinod and Jai were walking back towards them – shadows against the bright afternoon sunshine. Saif was speaking to Jai. '. . . it's not long until we become rich! Mrs Surya was saying how we'll soon be able to mine the moon and sell everything we find!' Saif saw Mrs Kajal and beamed, as if silver coins were about to pour from the skies that very second. 'Isn't that right, Mrs Kajal?'

Mrs Kajal bit her lip. The wind that had been rushing at them seemed to suddenly die down. As she spoke, her eyes were bleak. 'It depends what you mean, Saif. Historically, and in the present, colonizers use laws as spells, and maps as magic. They say they own a piece of the planet, they put a flag on it, and they do – no matter the rights of indigenous people, or the effects on animals, or vegetation. Now we're trying to do the same in space. Is it "possible" to sell what we mine on the moon? Legally, I think the answer is yes. Is it "right"? I truly don't know.'

Saif looked at her in confusion. Mrs Kajal shook her head, as if trying to clear it. Ajay looked at her with interest.

'The wind's changing. We should leave now if I – and my co-pilot – are going to get you all back to Jaipur,' said Anita, coming over to them. Her eyes bubbled with warm laughter when she saw Yasmin's delight at being named 'co-pilot'.

As they rushed down the stairs, Yasmin and Vinod far ahead of him, Ajay decided not to worry about the sore feeling in his chest. After all, being excited about flying was one thing – but the stakes for the latest story for *The Mumbai Sun* were beyond sky-high: they went all the way to the moon!

Yasmin would see it the same way.

Ajay was sure of it.

31

That evening, back at the hotel, the concierge motioned to Ajay and the others as they came through the intricately carved marble doors. With a flourish, he showed Ajay a silver platter with a note on it.

Ajay picked up the note, read it and grinned. 'It's an invitation from Laxmi to see the workshop!'

The evening air was warm and relaxing after the chilly air-conditioned insides of the space centre. As they walked through the dusty-pink city to get to the workshop, Ajay went back over his notes in his head. Mrs Surya had been definite that they could not let anyone know about the sabotage attempts until the saboteur was caught.

Saif was brimming with confidence as he spoke to Yasmin and Jai.

'Have no fear! I will discover the saboteur in our investigations tomorrow,' he said as they walked together. 'And, when I do, Mrs Surya will employ me as the chief engineer for the Space Programme.'

Yasmin smiled. Jai put his hand on Saif's shoulder in support.

Ajay was walking with Vinod, slightly behind the others. It was now or never! Ajay took a deep breath and rolled out the speech he had rehearsed.

'Vinod bhai,' he began formally, as they walked. 'Please forgive me for not including you straight away in Mrs Surya's meeting. I am editor of *The Mumbai Sun*. I had to consider losing access to Mrs Surya and—'

'Stop, Ajay,' Vinod said tiredly.

Ajay stopped.

'I understand why you and Saif didn't include me straight away,' Vinod said.

Ajay relaxed. He should have known Vinod would! They were friends. They were family!

Vinod looked at him.

'I understand it,' Vinod repeated.

'I thought you—' Ajay began happily.

'I just can't forgive you for it,' Vinod cut in softly.

Ajay stood still. Vinod's words reverberated through him. Each one like a knife.

'Remember how Mahesh used to hit me at the restaurant?' Vinod's voice was strained. 'The other workers thought that because Mahesh was good *to them,* he was a good person. They thought I should put up with being treated differently. You were my friend Ajay, but when Mrs Surya included you and asked you to think about excluding me, you did. How can you be my friend after that?'

Vinod looked as if he was about to say something else. His face was hollow and filled with sadness. But instead he walked swiftly away from Ajay to join the others.

Jai looking back, and seeing Ajay rooted to the spot, waved him over, his gold eyes sparkling.

'Hurry up, Ajay!' he called. 'We're here.'

Feeling sick at Vinod's words, Ajay walked slowly over to where they were all standing.

Vinod couldn't mean it, he thought feverishly. *They had to still be friends.*

Ajay watched as Yasmin knocked loudly on the wooden door of the warehouse they had been to earlier. No one answered. She frowned. Motioning to them all to be careful, she twisted the door handle.

There was a sharp click. It was unlocked!

She pushed the wooden door open, and they entered. Jai gripped his new cricket bat; Vinod held up his saucepan, the crack from the drone attack still visible.

Ajay followed them all into the darkness. The room was pitch black, as if colour and light had drained from the world. He reached blindly for the others. For Vinod. But although he knew they were there, he couldn't see or touch them.

Ajay felt panic rising in his throat.

Then the lights switched on. The room blazed with warmth and Laxmi and the Jaipur kids ran over to hug them, shouting joyfully.

'Surprise!'

32

Ajay breathed to calm himself down. It was a surprise party to thank them for the prize money. The Jaipur kids had fashioned party hats out of scrolls of newspaper, put up a large banner (a white sheet, perhaps stolen from a washing line) with 'Thank you!!!!!!' painted on it in bold letters and hung festive tissue-paper lanterns around the workshop. Ajay's heart burnt in his chest.

He loved parties (the railway kids in Mumbai had big, noisy ones at Diwali and Eid, with lots of firecrackers) but how could he enjoy this one – or any party ever again – if Vinod was not his friend?

'Let me show you around!' said Laxmi. She

looked free
and happy as if
invisible concrete
slabs had been taken
off her shoulders.

Ajay slowly followed her. Even weighed down with guilt, he could see that the warehouse had been transformed with the prize money. It smelt of fresh paint and varnish, and the cream and terracotta walls gleamed in the warm lamplight. Laxmi and the Jaipur kids proudly showed off the brand-new machinery that could cut and burnish metal and polish stones until they dazzled.

Laxmi brought out a tin box, which she unlocked. 'Prototypes for the first designs,' she said shyly. Inside, along with the pendant she had shown them earlier, were hanging silver earrings with dangling crescent moons. Yasmin gasped and immediately put them against her ears, looking radiant. She gave them back carefully. 'They're beautiful!' she said. 'You're going to be rich!'

Laxmi shook her head. She stared at her hand, and the stump where her finger had been. 'Only if we can sell them. The factory where we used to work bribes the tourist guides. All the tourists are taken there.'

Ajay took out his notebook and pen. It would take time to make things right with Vinod; this he could solve *now*. 'We'll make them see how dangerous it is to work there!'

'Ajay,' Yasmin warned, reading his mind. 'Remember the T-shirt factory!'

'It's different!' insisted Ajay. 'People at the factory won't go hungry. They can work here instead.' He turned to Laxmi. 'Don't worry, Laxmi! We'll write a story for *The Mumbai Sun* exposing the owner. They'll go to prison!'

Laxmi grabbed his arm. 'No – Ajay, listen. Leave it. The owner is too dangerous.'

'You know who it is?' asked Jai, his gold eyes fierce.

Laxmi's face froze.

She did know who it was! She was just too

frightened to say! Ajay seethed with anger. *The Mumbai Sun* would bring the owner to justice. He glanced at Vinod and saw the same resolve in his eyes. Vinod nodded slightly at Ajay. They might not be friends (*temporarily!* Ajay promised himself) but they both were united on this.

Just then, they heard fizzing and crackles and explosions from outside.

The girl with blue hair, who had helped Vinod make tea the last time they were there, burst in. She was trembling, barely able to speak because of the excitement that seemed to spark from her hair and fingertips. 'Have you heard the news?' She pointed outside, where the noise of the crowd was like a rocket launcher.

Ajay and the others rushed out. It felt like everyone in Jaipur – people who could be teachers, sugarcane juice sellers, cleaners, tiffin makers, bookbinders, builders, shop owners, glassblowers, umbrella painters, stonecutters, kachori fryers, waiters, cleaners, gardeners, growers, cloth dyers, rainmakers, number crunchers, wheeler-dealers, writers, rickshaw drivers, AI designers, transcendence seekers, investors, political speakers – had stepped out and were gazing at the rose-petal sky. A plane was scrawling words in white plumes of bubble writing in the sky. 'Anita! India's Chosen Astronaut to the Moon!'

The sound of applause and cheers rang out at her name.

Anita, their friend, the pilot, was now the most famous person in India!

She had been picked out of more than a billion people to fly WECU's rocket to the moon!

Ajay's heart beat like tabla at a wedding. The moon landing would be like a Bollywood film! He could see it now: Anita would land her moon mobile on its surface, jump out – with a giant leap for humankind! – and look back at Earth: a single, delicate figure, with a turquoise scarf peeping out from under her helmet and eyes that blazed with excitement.

Ajay's heart soared!

From the rooftops above him, interrupting his flight of imagination, fireworks whistled upwards in dazzling streams and curtains of light. Rockets pierced the sky and shattered in a million ruby, emerald and golden raindrops. Platinum-bright light swirled upwards. Firecrackers snapped and popped as they hit the concrete. The streets smelt of smoky gunpowder, halwa and raw sugar. People who wouldn't normally look at each other were spinning each other around in abandon. Someone had put on speakers. Kids danced Bollywood steps to the rollicking music thrumming through the streets, babies clapped their hands to the beat of tabla and old men and women hit their walking sticks in time on the ground. Even the Jaipur kids were creating bhangra dance moves.

Separating themselves slightly from the celebrations, Ajay, Yasmin, Jai, Saif, Vinod and Laxmi stood in a circle. Unable to help himself, Ajay took out the map that the saboteur had marked. Seeing it, they all grew still and silent. Yasmin's eyes were wide. 'You know what this means don't you, Ajay?' she whispered.

Thinking about Anita and her vividly laughing face above her turquoise scarf, Ajay nodded, the paper crackling in his hand. His earlier mood of exuberance gone, he now felt grim with anxiety. This was no longer just about the story, or even the Space Programme.

'We have to find the saboteur before they sabotage the rocket because otherwise . . .' he began.

'Anita's life will be at stake,' Yasmin finished,
staring at the map as if it were a snake.

33

It was very quiet in the astronaut training facility.

'Are you sure about this, Ajay?' Yasmin asked. 'Shouldn't we wait until Mrs Surya knows we're here?'

'We want to catch the saboteur, don't we?' said Ajay, trying to find the light switch with his torch. 'The early worm catches the bird!'

'That's what I'm worried about,' murmured Yasmin.

It was four in the morning. After getting back from the warehouse, Ajay had rung Rikesh, the Rickshaw driver with the moustache. He had come at once to the hotel and driven them all through the night (they had slept, huddled together, in the back) to the glass fortress walls of the space centre, leaving them there with warm wishes and more garlands of tinsel. Due to the top-level clearance Mrs Surya had given them, Ajay had walked the others straight through security. Vinod had gone to the food laboratory to see if he could find any clues from the first sabotage attempt. Yasmin, Saif and Jai had followed Ajay (who had the map) in darkness to the training facility.

'Got them!' Ajay said, finding the panel of switches. He flicked them all on.

The training facility was instantly flooded with white light. Ajay gasped. In the centre was the biggest swimming pool he had ever seen. It must be the biggest pool in India! The water was a deep, deep oily blue-black in the lights.

'Do astronauts like doing laps?' Jai asked, astonished.

Yasmin shook her head. 'I think it's to practise using the space suit and doing repairs in micro-gravity conditions. Floating in water is a lot like floating in space.'

At their look of surprise, she shrugged. 'I

researched "How to be an astronaut" on the hotel computer.'

Ajay felt a stab of loneliness. First a pilot, now an astronaut? What would he do if Yasmin left *The Mumbai Sun* and went to space without him?

He shivered. He had to focus! The team had to discover the saboteur before Anita got hurt.

'It's a crime scene,' said Yasmin, looking around. 'We just need to find the exact scene of the crime.'

'It's not the only one,' Saif reminded them. 'Where's the engine room, Ajay?'

Ajay consulted the map. 'Through there,' he said, and pointed at the doors on the other side of the training facility.

'I shall go at once. An engine is a very complicated piece of machinery. It will take time to check it,' said Saif grandly. Then he became stern. 'But even an apprentice engineer cannot do this alone.' He started to count off on his fingers. 'I'll need one person to hold the torch and another to hold the tools—'

'Aren't I already doing that?' asked Jai, his arm muscles flexing as he moved Saif's over-stuffed

174

suitcase of tools from one hand to the other (Saif had asked him to carry it for a moment as they got off the rickshaw and, for some reason, had not yet claimed it back).

Saif waved away the interruption '—and to help me balance. The engine is very high up,' he added.

Ajay took out Mr Gupta's notebook and pen, and made a decision. 'Let's split up. You three check out the engine room, I'll investigate here.'

The others nodded and raced off.

And for the first time since they had got to Jaipur, Ajay was completely alone.

It was time to get the story for *The Mumbai Sun*!

He had seen TV shows about investigating crime scenes. Investigating required logic, a methodical process, rational thinking! He would begin the same way. Ajay frowned and thought hard.

If he were a saboteur, what would he do?

Ajay looked at the swimming pool. The pool water was very still. Ajay could see his reflection on the glossy surface. Suddenly he felt sad that he had never learnt how to swim. It must feel wonderful to see a swimming pool and know you could dive through its deep-blue surface and splash around, and feel the silky wet water against your skin.

Did swimmers think differently as they moved through water? Was that why Yasmin wanted to fly? So that she could glide through air and swim through stars? And feel free?

Ajay bit his lip, knelt and dipped his hand in the cool water.

Memories caught at him – his mother taking him to Chowpatty beach, running with him into the sea, laughing with him as they tried to jump out of the way before the white surf rushed in and bubbled over their feet. He could still smell the salt of sea spray, hear the squelching of wet sand in between his toes – feel the calluses on her hand as she wrapped her fingers firmly around his.

Ajay's chest grew tight. How could she have left him?

And if his mother had left him, of course Vinod and Yasmin could leave him too.

He stood up quickly, the water falling from his hand in cold droplets as he wiped it on his shirt. He would examine the rest of the pool later, when he didn't feel his heart had just been cut in two.

He looked around.

And then he spotted it.

The first place where – if he wanted to destroy the Space Programme by hurting its chosen astro-naut – he would commit the act of sabotage.

34

It was a machine with a central pole, on the other side of the training facility. It had a long mechanical arm (like the arm of a crane on a building site) and, on the end of the arm, a white spherical capsule that looked like a pod. The capsule's door had been swung wide open.

Sticking his pen behind his ear, Ajay warily walked towards the capsule and stuck his head around the open door.

The capsule was padded, with a chair and a computer. It must be an astronaut training machine!

Ajay clambered in.

He started to search for something that looked

out of place.

It took less than a minute to find the broken seat belt.

'How could someone do this?' he whispered out loud, horrified. The seat belt was meant to be in two parts on either side of the chair, which Anita could clasp together once she had sat down – but whilst one half was still attached to the seat, most of the other half had been wrenched away from it, so that only the tiniest sliver of its strap still remained.

Ajay clenched his fists, boiling with fury. How *dare* someone do this?

He imagined Anita getting into the machine, closing the door behind her, sitting in the seat, and only then realizing that the belt had been damaged.

What if the machine had started before she could warn the operators?

She could have died!

This wasn't just someone willing to commit an act of sabotage – it was someone willing to commit *murder*.

He had to find out who had done this.

Ajay took out the magnifying glass Laxmi had fashioned for him and peered through it, gasping in astonishment. Seeing the sliver of strap that had been left, close-up, was as good as seeing far-off planets! He could see every detail – and with every detail came new information. The strap hadn't been wrenched away from the sliver that remained – it had been hacked away! The clean slashes showed that some sort of serrated blade had been used. A rushed job by a person who hadn't realized how tough the strap would be. They hadn't had time to cut through it properly. He could tell from the way the slashes gave way to rip marks at the end.

Where was the part of the strap that had been cut away?

Ajay got on his hands and knees to search. There was a sound of footsteps outside.

'Yasmin! Over here!' he shouted.

He couldn't find anything on the ground. The saboteur must have taken it. The capsule was getting darker. He looked up. That was strange: the wedge of light on the wall from the open door of the capsule was becoming smaller.

And where exactly was Yasmin?

Ajay turned and looked behind him. The capsule door was closing.

He jumped up.

Too late.

The capsule door slammed shut just as he reached it.

He tried to open it – but it was locked.

He was trapped!

35

Ajay rattled the handle of the capsule door again. No use! It wouldn't budge!

'Help!'

He hammered the door with his fists.

'Yasmin! Vinod! Help!'

His voice was raw, his fists red as he hit the door again and again.

'Jai! Saif!'

It didn't matter. The padded insides were just absorbing the shock.

'Please, help!'

It was no good! There was no one there. He turned around, exhausted, his back to the door, and slid to the ground. How could he have let himself get trapped like this?

He breathed. He had to stay calm and wait for the others to rescue him. After all, things could be . . .

The capsule started to move.

. . . worse!

Ajay scrambled to his feet.

The capsule was moving in a circular path. But it was very gentle – almost like the fairground ride he had been on once in Mumbai.

This isn't so bad! he thought with relief. *Perhaps Anita hadn't been in as much danger as he had thought.*

It went a little faster.

Ajay felt the air whip at his hair and his face.

And faster.

He put up his arm against the invisible force. It threw him against the closed door. The metal doorknob jammed into his back, sending agonizing waves ricocheting through his spine. Ajay cried out. This was no fairground ride. It was like being spun so fast in a bucket that water stayed inside. His eyes watered as the force of the spinning kept him pinned to the wall of the capsule.

He was helpless.

The force was crushing him.

He would not find his mother; he would not write his story; he would not see Yasmin become a pilot.

And – worst of all – he would not see Vinod again.

Tears crowded in his eyes, only to be immediately ripped away by the spinning force.

Vinod.

He had relied on Vinod's friendship all his life. And then he had thrown it away.

The capsule went faster and faster.

Ajay closed his eyes.

Now he would never get a chance to mend their friendship.

His heart throbbed violently in his chest.

And then . . .

just when there was no hope left

. . . he felt the speed of the capsule change.

It started to slow down.

Slower and slower and slower

– and slow –

. . . until finally it ground to a halt.

Ajay fell forward from the wall, collapsed on

the floor of the capsule and vomited.

Dizzy and sick, he heard the door to the capsule being ripped open, heard someone come in.

He looked up weakly. Vinod's thin face was filled with terror as he ran up to him, knelt and held him. 'I heard you shouting for Yasmin and saw a figure running away. I tried to stop the machine, but nothing was working, until—'

Ajay threw his arms around his friend.

Vinod's arms were around him, steadying him.

'I'm sorry,' Ajay whispered.

'Stop, Ajay,' said Vinod. There was a crack in his voice.

They embraced each other tightly as Ajay cried into Vinod's shoulder.

36

Vinod helped Ajay out of the capsule. Ajay wobbled once or twice – he was seeing double of everything, including the door! – but each time Vinod caught and steadied him, and let Ajay lean his aching head against his shoulder. As Ajay fell, exhausted, into a chair outside, Vinod got a bottle of water and helped him clean up.

Finally feeling better, Ajay looked up. Vinod (just one of him, now that Ajay was no longer seeing double!) was standing next to him, holding the open bottle of water, his eyes creased with concern. Over Vinod's shoulder, Ajay could see the control panel of the capsule. Its buttons were flashing in bright neon colours, and scissors of silver light were sparking and crackling wildly from where Vinod's saucepan had been jammed into it.

Ajay gulped.

'You saved my life,' he said. And then, because he had no other words, 'Thank you.'

Vinod's eyes misted up. He nodded.

Saif burst in through the doors and saw them. 'Why are you relaxing?' he asked Ajay accusingly, standing in front of them. 'This is not the time to put your feet up!' Then he beamed. 'Whilst you two have been taking it easy and doing nothing, I, Saif, apprentice engineer, have found the sabotage device on the engine! Of course,' he added magnanimously as Yasmin and Jai came in through the door, 'I could not have done it without my two assistants.'

Yasmin and Jai had stopped short and were staring in shock at the control panel, with Vinod's saucepan sticking out of it.

'The saboteur had stuck a remote-control explosion device on to the engine. It was very easy for me to find and defuse,' Saif continued, oblivious of the saucepan. He held up a device with lots of wires spiralling from it. 'Almost too easy for an apprentice engineer of my ability,' he added grandly. 'The saboteur has clearly underestimated who they are dealing with!'

'Do you know who did it?' asked Ajay.

Saif shook his head. 'But whoever it is, is nearby. The remote control only works at a range of twenty metres.'

'Twenty metres?' There was the sound of clapping and Mrs Surya's voice behind them. 'Well done, Saif! I knew I could rely on you!'

Ajay turned to look at her as she came in. Her hair was coiled over one shoulder and she glittered in a sari embroidered with moss-green stones that sparkled like emeralds in the light. As she entered, a flurry of people in dark suits and carrying clipboards came in around her. Ignoring them, Mrs Surya stepped forward, put her hand on Saif's shoulder and smiled. She was about to say something when her smile froze. Ajay followed her gaze. She was staring at Vinod's saucepan, which was now glowing with white light and had clearly destroyed the control panel.

Ajay hurriedly explained. 'The saboteur damaged

the seat belt in the capsule – then tried to kill me. Vinod saved me with his saucepan.'

Yasmin gasped and looked at him, her face turning pale with shock. 'I'm fine,' Ajay reassured her.

Mrs Surya's mouth dropped. 'The saboteur tried to kill you? In *my* space centre? Did you see who it was?'

Vinod shook his head. 'Whoever it was, was too far away.'

'So the saboteur is still here?' Mrs Surya looked grim. Her eyes narrowed. 'It is time to put a stop to this and protect you and the space programme once and for all. You want your story, Ajay? It is time to get it. Follow me.'

Ajay jumped off his seat and took Mr Gupta's notebook and pen out. This, and his near escape from death (now that he had definitely escaped it), would make the finest story *The Mumbai Sun* had ever seen!

He and the others followed Mrs Surya as she swept through doors, through the engine room and into the room they had been in the day before. Ajay frowned as Mrs Surya approached Mrs Kajal's desk and, taking a set of keys from one of her entourage, started to open it.

Why was she doing that?

It couldn't be Mrs Kajal!

But Mrs Kajal did have a motive – she didn't agree with Mrs Surya's plans.

And only those with top-level security clearance – like the Chief Scientist – would have access to the rocket after the safety teams had passed through.

And her private desk was within twenty metres of the explosive device.

Ajay rubbed his head. Even if all that was true, surely they should only open her desk drawer if she was there?

'Are you allowed to do that?' he asked.

Mrs Surya looked at him, and her eyes were troubled. 'I understand why you are asking,' she said. 'Normally, not without proof. But national security is at stake. In those circumstances, individual rights can be put aside. I have had my suspicions about Mrs Kajal for a long time. Now is the time to find the proof to back them up.'

With a twist of her hand, she pulled open the drawer.

Ajay felt sick. Nestled inside, coiled like a snake, was the part of the seat belt that had been hacked away from the spinning capsule. Next to it was a remote control.

'Is it the remote control to the explosive device?' Mrs Surya turned and asked Saif.

Saif looked at it. All his blazing joy at finding the device had evaporated. He looked at Ajay, and in his eyes Ajay saw the weight of what he was about to say hit him. If he said 'Yes', Mrs Kajal would be arrested. If he said 'No' . . .

There was a long pause.

'Yes,' Saif whispered.

'Are you sure?' Mrs Surya asked softly. 'A lot rides on this.'

Saif nodded.

The doors to the lift on the opposite side of the room hissed open. Mrs Kajal, wearing a sea-blue sari and bracelets that chimed like bells, stepped in. She saw them, and her body tensed as if she was about to make a run for it.

Mrs Surya looked up. Her eyes flashed with fire. 'There's our saboteur! Get her!'

37

Five security guards leapt forward as if they had been trained for this moment. Two grabbed Mrs Kajal's arms and twisted them back, another got out handcuffs and two more surrounded her.

'Get off me.' Mrs Kajal struggled as the handcuffs were slapped on to her wrists.

Ajay stepped forward. 'Stop!' he shouted at the guards.

Mrs Surya gently put her hand on his shoulder. 'Ajay, you must understand the gravity of what Mrs Kajal has done,' she said. 'This isn't a normal situation. She doesn't deserve any rights after trying to sabotage the space centre and trying to murder you and Anita.'

Mrs Kajal, surrounded by the guards, was trembling like a water reed. At Mrs Surya's words, she opened her mouth – but couldn't speak. The guards tightened their hands on her arms.

Was Mrs Surya right? Mrs Kajal had been tricking them all along. She had been prepared to kill him! Why should he care about what happened to her now?

His heart hammered in his chest. He didn't understand. How could someone like Mrs Kajal, with her sharp sense of justice, do something like this?

Jai stepped forward, his gold eyes crackling, his face strained – the only one of them who knew what it was like to be in a prison cell. He rarely spoke of it, but even now he would shake when he passed the building where he had been held in Mumbai.

The guards were using force when there was no need. They were *enjoying* using it, even though they outnumbered her five to one.

Ajay spoke sharply. 'She still has rights. *The Mumbai Sun* will defend them.'

Mrs Surya's eyes flickered. 'Even though she

tried to murder you?'

Ajay buried the terror of the spinning capsule and turned to a fresh page in his notebook. He clicked on Mr Gupta's ballpoint pen. 'Even then.'

Mrs Surya gave him a long, cool look. Then she sighed. 'Very well, Ajay. Since you asked.' She gestured to the guards, who released their hold on Mrs Kajal. 'Escort her to a secure room until the police get here. I hope that you're satisfied, Ajay.'

As she was hustled out, Mrs Kajal turned to Ajay, her hands clenched together in distress.

'Get her out of here now,' commanded Mrs Surya.

'The Minutes, Ajay!' Mrs Kajal gasped as the guards took her past him, in a voice so strained that he could barely catch the words. 'Find the Minutes!'

'Now!' shouted Mrs Surya.

And before Ajay could ask her anything more, Mrs Kajal was hurriedly bundled away.

38

Mrs Surya had called a press conference at the space centre. A selection of the press in Jaipur were there, buzzing with anticipation, but so were crowds of people who were clearly not journalists and had been brought in, Ajay assumed, to swell numbers. Ajay and his friends were in a special, exclusive area, cordoned off especially for *The Mumbai Sun*.

Ajay waited with the others, holding Mr Gupta's pen and notebook in his hand. All he could think about were Mrs Kajal's last words. 'Find the minutes,' she had said. What did she mean? And why minutes – and not hours, or days?

Ajay squirmed in the heat. Ever since Mrs Kajal's arrest that morning, he had alternated between feeling ice cold and feeling hot and bothered and itchy all over. He had rung Lata, his lawyer friend in Mumbai, to make sure that Mrs Kajal was treated well in prison, where she would be held until the first court hearing next year. What else could he do?

While they waited for Mrs Surya to appear, waiters were coming round with glasses of pale green sugarcane juice and pink crushed watermelon juice. On platters were packets of freeze-dried ice cream. Ajay took one and unwrapped it.

He went through the evidence in his head again. The map, the tampered food (Vinod had reported back that it had been obvious which packets had been tampered with during the first sabotage attempt), the broken seat belt, the explosive. It all pointed to Mrs Kajal's guilt.

Absently, he bit into the ice cream. And almost spat it out. It was not cold, but it was very sweet and crumbly – and tasted like biting into cardboard. If Anita was going into space, Vinod needed to work on some recipes to send her that she could eat properly!

The evidence was all too convenient.

Ajay stared at the rest of the freeze-dried ice cream, his thoughts whirring. It looked like real ice cream, it was more convenient than real ice cream – and yet it didn't taste like the real thing.

Why would Mrs Kajal – the person who knew the space centre better than anyone – need a map marked with crosses to plan the sabotage? Why would the *Chief Scientist of the entire Space Programme* cut a seat belt and plant an explosive to sabotage it? Surely she had the skills to secretly dismantle entire rockets if she wanted to?

Nothing about the evidence hung together. And Lata

had said with disgust that Mrs Kajal's access to lawyers was limited because her alleged crime was a national security concern. For there to be any chance of getting to the truth, *The Mumbai Sun* needed to be the one to investigate further!

He opened his mouth to speak to the others, when Saif elbowed him in the stomach – Ajay choked, puffing out air.

'Look!' Saif's eyes were starry as he looked up at the stage, quivering with excitement. Mrs Surya was on the podium, dressed in a silver sari that looked as if it were made from woven moonbeams. 'The press conference – it's about to begin!'

39

Mrs Surya smiled at the crowd from the podium. 'Thank you for gathering here today at such short notice.' Then she grew serious. 'I will not waste your time. I have news. It is news that will shock and horrify you. *The Mumbai Sun* – the newspaper that uncovered corruption in Mumbai – has just discovered a saboteur in our midst!'

Ajay became still. Why hadn't she waited until the investigations were complete?

The crowd collectively sucked in their breath.

'And, what is worse, the alleged saboteur is the very person appointed to oversee the entire WECU Programme. She has used her voting rights multiple times in the past to block our plans to transform the future. But even that hasn't been enough. Envious of a future that will owe more to AI and technology than scientists, she has now tried to block progress and destroy the Space Programme itself! Thanks to the work of *The Mumbai Sun*, whose integrity cannot be questioned, I can finally disclose to you that the alleged saboteur is none other than . . . Mrs Kajal!'

There was a moment of shock.

Ajay tried to shout, 'Wait! It's more complicated than that!' but the crowd had started jeering too loudly for him to be heard; an elderly journalist whacked the floor with a cane in fury. Jai stood up, creating a protective barrier between them and the crowd. Ajay was glad of him nearby. He could feel the crowd whipping itself up into a frenzy of outrage.

'This is what comes of having women scientists,' shouted someone from the corner.

Yasmin looked sick. Jai's eyes kindled with anger.

Ajay felt disgust rising in his throat. It didn't

take much for people's prejudices to ignite.

Mrs Surya spoke again through her mic. 'You will be glad to hear that Mrs Kajal has been arrested—'

There were cheers and whoops from all around them.

'They've already decided she's guilty,' whispered Vinod. 'Without hearing her side.'

'Hadn't we decided that too?' murmured Jai, his gold eyes dark with self-recrimination.

'I think Mrs Kajal's alleged treachery proves what I have always said,' Mrs Surya continued. 'Entrepreneurs should have complete freedom when it comes to exploring space!' There were cheers and claps from the crowd. Ajay, remembering the lukewarm response Mrs Surya had got to the same suggestion at the awards ceremony, marvelled at how quickly she had won them over.

'And now, for the biggest news of all.'

She paused, and Ajay saw her eyes light up.

'Following Mrs Kajal's arrest, I present to you a new partner for the WECU Space Programme: an international conglomerate which, unlike Mrs Kajal, supports my dream to colonize space. It is a company that specializes in technology, and its surveillance ware will be sent to space in two days' time with our rocket. We're lucky enough to have the company's CEO with us today. He has travelled from abroad to see us. Please put your hands together for him – the CEO of The Four.'

The CEO went up on stage to stand next to her.

The crowd went wild – clapping and cheering loud enough that the replica of the satellite Aryabhata, poised precariously above them, looked as if it was about to tip and fall.

Instinctively, Ajay, Yasmin, Vinod, Jai and Saif linked hands, as if by holding on to each other they could protect themselves from the horror of what they were seeing on stage.

The CEO who Mrs Surya had called up to stand with her was none other than The Man in the Grey Suit.

40

A second later, Ajay was running towards the podium, with the incredible speed of the footballers from Japan he had seen on the television. He had to convince Mrs Surya that partnering up with The Man in the Grey Suit was a terrible mistake!

He was blocked by Mrs Surya's security guards.

'I'm Ajay, editor of *The Mumbai Sun*—' Ajay began.

'Mrs Surya's instructions are that no one is allowed near the podium,' said one.

Ajay tried to shout out to her on stage, but Mrs Surya looked past him. The Man in the Grey Suit surveyed the crowd with his blue eyes sweeping over them like torches, his powerful build dominating the stage. Then, together with Mrs Surya and her entourage, he walked back off the stage into a private conference room.

The guard shoved Ajay backwards.

The crowd behind him, now being plied with champagne and chocolate dipped in gold leaf, was still jostling and cheering. Ajay tried to think clearly. What could he do next?

There was a whistle from the curtain near him. 'Ajay, Yasmin, Saif, Vinod, Jai – over here!' Anita shouted, her fingers to her lips, beckoning them over. With Mrs Surya gone and the guards and crowd jostling them from all sides, they ran towards her and through the curtain that Anita held open for them, into the corridor where she was standing waiting for them.

She let the curtain fall behind them.

The emptiness of the corridor and sudden hush was a relief after the hustle of the press conference.

'You looked like you needed some help,' said Anita, her arms crossed, her turquoise scarf wound around her throat like a ribbon of sky.

'I need a meeting with Mrs Surya,' said Ajay quickly. 'Can you find a way to get me to see her?'

'I can take you to her office. She'll be there in a few minutes. The CEO of The Four has left to get ready in his hotel. They're flying out by private jet this evening for dinner with a politician in Mumbai.'

'Flying?' squeaked Saif. Ajay wasn't sure whether it was from his fear of planes or his wish to go with them to the restaurant.

Anita nodded. 'They'll be back for the press conference tomorrow morning.'

'Another press conference?' asked Ajay in surprise. When were journalists meant to have any time to investigate anything?

'It's the day before the rocket launch. Journalists from all across India and around the world will be there.' Anita's usually vivid face looked carved of stone.

'You're not excited?' said Yasmin tentatively.

'Mrs Kajal's in prison,' Anita said, and her voice was sharp with grief. 'How can I be?'

'Even if she's been arrested for trying to kill you?' said Yasmin.

Anita shook her head. 'It wasn't her. I know it wasn't. She cared for us.'

Ajay digested the words and felt a ripple of fear. *The Mumbai Sun* had been responsible for Mrs Kajal's arrest. But Anita could be wrong. How was it possible to truly judge someone and know what they were like? 'When Mrs Kajal was arrested, she told me to "Find the minutes". What did she mean?'

Anita frowned, tapping her foot. 'Mrs Kajal and Mrs Surya had an emergency meeting yesterday. Could it be the Minutes from that?'

Ajay looked at her blankly.

'Minutes are written records of what is said in a meeting,' said Anita at his look of confusion. 'They're meant to keep people accountable. Mrs Kajal insisted that they were taken at every meeting she took part in at WECU. In any meetings I was invited to, Mrs Surya's secretary always wrote them by hand.'

He was about to ask her to explain in more detail, when the walls of the corridor went dark. Mrs Surya's face appeared on screen. Her voice was warm and welcoming. 'Ajay, are you still looking for me? If you are, I am free now. Why don't you come up to my office?'

The screen went blank.

'Was she listening to us?' whispered Yasmin.

'There's a rumour that these walls have ears,' said Anita slowly.

Ajay looked at the blank mirror-like surfaces of the walls in awe.

41

'Enter,' Mrs Surya called after Ajay had waited outside for fifteen minutes.

Ajay was alone – he had asked the team to come with him but Vinod and the others had shaken their heads, saying that he was more likely to convince Mrs Surya if he went on his own.

As Ajay entered, Mrs Surya had her back to him. She was following the glittering fish in the tank with her eyes. As he approached her, she turned.

They sat down on the chairs. There was a plate of sesame biscuits on the table. His favourite! Ajay took a few, snapped them and crammed them in his mouth, enjoying the sweet crackle and chewiness of them.

'What can I do for you, Ajay?' said Mrs Surya.

'It's The Man in the Grey Suit,' said Ajay, trying to get a bit of biscuit that had lodged in the back of his mouth with his tongue.

'Who?' Mrs Surya said, blinking.

Ajay leafed through the notebook. 'The CEO of The Four.'

'Ah.' Mrs Surya inclined her head. 'What about him?'

'He's dangerous. He stole Saif's suitcase and attacked me and my friends with drones when we were racing to get to the meteorite. You can't make him a partner of the Space Programme.'

Mrs Surya turned very still. 'Do you have any proof?'

'We saw him,' said Ajay.

'I'm afraid that's not quite enough,' said Mrs Surya, relaxing. She sat with liquid elegance. 'Whatever happened must have been some sort of misunderstanding.'

Ajay shook his head. He was about to show her the scar on his arm caused by the leg of the drone slicing into it – then he remembered that she already knew about it and that her doctor had looked after him.

'Let me share something with you, Ajay,' said Mrs Surya, and he felt himself relax into her confidence. 'The partnership with The Four is a huge prize – not just for WECU, but for India.' She looked directly at him – and in her eyes was a fierce light. 'The Four is an international company that can provide us with satellite surveillance technology beyond our wildest dreams. It will allow us to watch, unnoticed, all of our enemies and keep ourselves safe. Don't you want that, Ajay? To make sure that no one feels powerless in the way that we once did?'

Ajay tried to keep his thoughts together. 'But The Man in the Grey Suit attacked us!'

Mrs Surya clasped her hands together, and her voice was soothing. 'I think you must have misunderstood what happened. But if – and it's a big if – Ajay, you are right and he did attack you to try and win the race, surely you can see the bigger picture now? The Four will tip the balance in the battle for space, and on Earth as well. What are a few scratches compared to that?'

Ajay felt himself being won over.

Mrs Surya stood up and moved to the window, beckoning Ajay to come with her. They stood there, together, looking out at the acres of land rippling outwards from the space centre, at the line of trees, at sequins of lakes, at the line of buildings and warehouses just in the distance. Ajay marvelled. Even his room at the station in Mumbai didn't have a view like this!

'I built this, Ajay,' said Mrs Surya softly, her hand with the glittering diamond ring on her finger delicately placed on the window's edge. 'I grew up living by sewers and found a way to crawl up the ladder of success rung by rung. How? By remembering that the end always justifies the means.' There was a note of dry humour in her voice, and her smile, reflected in the window, was wry. 'Now, leaders of the world tremble when they receive my call.'

Ajay could believe it. She was extraordinary.

She turned to look at him, and in her eyes was heartfelt belief. 'Societies are judged by their success, their power and their wealth! And together The Four and I are going to create one of

211

the greatest societies on Earth.'

Ajay wanted to cheer.

Mrs Surya took a deep breath and smiled, and in her eyes was a well of tenderness. 'But forget The Four for the moment, Ajay. I have another proposition for you. A proposition that I want you to consider carefully.

'I want WECU to buy *The Mumbai Sun*.'

42

Ajay was stunned into silence.

Mrs Surya laughed with merriment at his shock. She radiated happiness as they went back to the chairs.

'Think about it, Ajay! Think about what you and I and *The Mumbai Sun*, with its reputation for being incorruptible, could achieve together! *The Mumbai Sun* would never lack for funds. You could buy printers – an entire newsroom even. You could carry out all the investigations you wanted! All I would ask in return is that you tell WECU's stories – explain to a new generation how, in today's society, it is the rich and wealthy who are being oppressed; show my vision for a new society; argue for why power needs to remain concentrated in the hands of those who know how to wield it!'

Ajay was trying to wrap his head around her words, when Mrs Surya leant forward. 'Ajay, think about it. You want to change the world, but your sphere of influence is limited. With my resources behind you, *The Mumbai Sun* could be the greatest media organization in the world.'

Her eyes sparkled. 'And there's more, Ajay. I have the power to project your image across the skies.' Her voice filled with gentle warmth. 'If your mother is still alive, I'll find her for you.'

Ajay stared at her. Her words slowly sunk in.

He leapt up. He wanted to cry. To dance! Mrs Surya was able to do what she said. He knew enough of her power to understand that.

He would finally see his mother again.

Ajay hid his face, his vision blurring with unshed tears.

Mr Gupta's notebook fell from his hand.

After all this time – would his mother still remember what he looked like?

It was time to join forces with WECU and find her.

Dazzling emotions whirled through him. He needed to regain control and thank Mrs Surya for her kindness without bursting into tears!

He bent to pick up the notebook where it had opened on the back page—

'The job of a newspaper is to afflict the comfortable and comfort the afflicted.'

The quote had been jotted down on the back page in Mr Gupta's handwriting in a hurried splutter of ink.

Ajay slowly read the quote again.

And again.

His heart stopped beating.

For a moment he wished that he could push away the notebook. He wished that he could wash away the words from his mind and quickly accept Mrs Surya's offer.

But it was too late. The words burnt.

How had he forgotten what it meant to be a journalist? To afflict the comfortable and comfort the afflicted was the job of *The Mumbai Sun*. It was its *only* job.

If he accepted Mrs Surya's offer, and became her mouthpiece, he would see his mother again—

But it would only be by betraying everything that he believed in.

Ajay read the quote in Mr Gupta's notebook again, as if it were an anchor in a storm. And felt his heart break at the choice he was going to make.

'I can't,' Ajay said quietly.

'Excuse me?' Mrs Surya looked startled.

'I can't,' Ajay repeated, still reeling. 'My dream is to be a journalist and to listen to, and tell, the truth. Not to be a mouthpiece of the rich and powerful, but to hold them – you, even – to account.'

It didn't matter if a society was successful or powerful or wealthy. All that mattered was how it treated its most vulnerable.

He turned to a blank page in Mr Gupta's note-book, and clicked the ballpoint pen, unable to stop the crack in his voice. 'Thank you for your offer. But *The Mumbai Sun* isn't for sale.'

Mrs Surya looked as if she had just eaten an ice cube. All her warmth vanished.

'You understand that I won't be able to help you find your mother if you do not accept?'

Ajay felt his heart throb painfully in his chest.

He touched Mr Gupta's notebook to draw strength from it. How had he not seen it before? Gifts given, with no expectation of anything in return, were expressions of friendship. Those with strings attached were nothing more than bribes.

Ajay nodded, staring at the notebook, unable to speak.

'How dare you?' Mrs Surya whispered.

Ajay looked up, stunned.

'You blather on about the truth as if it mattered. Power doesn't come from truth, or knowledge, or compassion,' Mrs Surya hissed, her face contorted with sudden rage. 'Raw power, built from the plunder and exploitation of resources, is about being ruthless, hypocritical, even ignorant, and *still* being able to crush those around you without a second's thought.'

Ajay sat in silent horror.

Vinod had seen through Mrs Surya before any of them. He had judged her by paying attention to how she treated people she had power over.

'Very well.' Mrs Surya had regained control and her mask of civility had once again dropped over her features. Her voice was crisp and bone-shatteringly cold. She looked at the slim crystal dial on her wrist. 'And now, Ajay, I am sure you understand that time is precious.' She stood up.

Ajay did the same.

He let her usher him to the door, gathering himself and his thoughts, and it was just at the last moment that he turned.

'Mrs Kajal told me to "Find the Minutes" from your meeting with her. Do you have them?' It was a long shot. Ajay saw Mrs Surya suck in her breath sharply. For a moment, he thought she would just throw him out, but then she smiled, her eyes flickering.

'What if I said no? What would you do then?'

Ajay clicked on Mr Gupta's pen and opened up the notebook to a fresh page. 'I would ask readers of *The Mumbai Sun* to question "Why?",' he said carefully. 'Mrs Kajal asked for the Minutes to be taken at every meeting. Why would this be any different?'

Mrs Surya looked unconcerned.

Ajay thought quickly and switched tactics: 'Would it be possible to speak to your secretary?'

Mrs Surya's eyes gleamed. 'I am afraid you have just missed her. A few minutes ago, she left to go on a flight.'

Ajay made a show of writing her words down. 'I think the readers of *The Mumbai Sun* will find that interesting,' he murmured.

Mrs Surya smiled and shook her head. 'You don't need to write an article, Ajay. As it happens, I do have the Minutes. I'm actually surprised it took you so long to ask.' She went to her desk, unlocked it with an intricate green-gold key and, after a moment, brought out the two pages.

'Here they are. Now go. And Ajay?'

Ajay turned to face her.

Mrs Surya's voice was cool. 'You had the world

at your feet today, and you said no. No one ever says no to me without paying a price.'

Ajay let the door swing shut between them. For a moment he felt chilled by her words.

Then he squared his shoulders.

Mrs Surya thought that fear was a good substitute for respect. She didn't realize that there was a key difference.

Fear could be conquered.

43

Saif's eyes stared at him through the eye-shaped cut-out in the newspaper he was holding. He looked aggrieved. 'Why are we here again?'

They were seated in the reception area of the hotel where The Man in the Grey Suit was staying, which was somehow even more luxurious than their own, trying to look inconspicuous in their disguises as the other guests came in and out.

'Shh!' said Ajay, pushing down the fedora hat that Laxmi had found for him. He looked like a detective from a black and white movie! (Or he would if the hat didn't keep falling over his eyes.) 'You know why, Saif! To find proof!'

After Ajay's meeting with Mrs Surya, he had

recounted what had happened to the others. He had shown them the copy of the Minutes: notes of the meeting between Mrs Kajal and Mrs Surya detailing what each one had said.

'There's nothing here that helps Mrs Kajal,' Yasmin had said, reading the two sheets of paper. 'All that they talk about is the date of the rocket launch!'

Yasmin was right. So why had Mrs Kajal been so insistent that Ajay find them? And why, according to Anita, had Mrs Surya's secretary, who had been at the meeting with Mrs Surya and Mrs Kajal and written the Minutes, been transferred by Mrs Surya to the Maldives *that afternoon*?

With no other leads on the sabotage, *The Mumbai Sun* had only one option left – to investigate The Man in the Grey Suit!

Which was why Ajay and Saif were now sitting on plush grey sofas in the reception of his hotel.

'There he is!' shouted Saif.

'Shh!' Ajay clapped his hand over Saif's mouth. They watched as The Man in the Grey Suit, with his smoky eyes and loose, relaxed gait, like a bear's after a kill, deposited a scrolled silver key at the front desk.

'Room 101?' the concierge asked.

The Man in the Grey Suit nodded.

Ajay and Saif watched as he walked across the reception and out of the revolving doors with a chauffeur who had been waiting for him.

'We're in luck, Saif!' whispered Ajay in glee. 'He'll be gone for hours. Let's go!'

Saif folded up his newspaper and they hurried past the marble stairs at the side of the front desk to the ornate gilt and wrought-iron lift. 'First floor, please,' Ajay said to Dev, the bellboy, who was wearing a name tag that said 'Dev (he/ him)', and a sharp red and gold suit. Scribbling down some lines of poetry that he was reciting under his breath in his notebook, Dev looked irritable at being disturbed. He pressed a button. The antique lift, with its see-through ribbed walls, clanked and creaked as it lurched up to the first floor. They stepped out and padded along the corridor until they reached the door of room 101.

Saif got out two copper prongs from his bag.

'You're sure you can break in with those?' asked Ajay.

Saif gave him a withering stare. 'I am an apprentice engineer. I should, at this precise moment, be working on a space rocket. I am more than capable of unlocking a door.'

He put up his hand as Ajay began to protest and continued calmly. 'I do not wish to hear your excuses. I am only here to find proof about The Man in the Grey Suit so that Mrs Surya will trust us and allow us back into the space centre. Now please be quiet and keep a lookout so that I can work in peace.'

Ajay sighed.

The rest of the team had shared Ajay's misgivings over Mrs Surya. Saif, however, had been inconsolable – convinced that Ajay had made a terrible mistake in saying no to her.

It would be years before Saif let him hear the end of it.

Ajay kept his back to the door and settled down to watch the corridor, screening Saif as best as he could. His mind drifted. Who were the other guests staying here? They were in one of India's most prestigious hotels, after all!

One of the other room's doors opened. Ajay's

jaw dropped. It couldn't be! Could it? It was! His favourite NBA player! Even railway kids in Mumbai knew about him and his shooting! The tall NBA player grinned at Ajay as he walked past carrying a basketball. At one point he threw a scrunched-up bit of rubbish into a wastepaper bin at the other end of the corridor. Ajay imagined the swish!

Ajay rubbed his eyes.

Next down the corridor was an Asian actress known for her martial arts films and Oscar-worthy performances, who walked with panther-like grace and strength. Ajay had seen her in the movies he had sneaked into, doing death-defying stunts. She nodded as Ajay tipped his hat.

This was the best people-watching corridor in the world!

Down the corridor hurried a legendary Hollywood actor, with crooked teeth and a furrowed brow, carrying a worn copy of *Julius Caesar* by Shakespeare.

Ajay stared after him.

There was a click behind him. 'I have opened the lock,' Saif informed him in tones of infinite patience, as he turned around. 'You should hurry – unless, of course, you want to lose this opportunity as well?'

Ajay rolled his eyes.

44

Saif switched on the lights. The room was even larger than the ones Ajay had insisted they move out of at their own hotel to go and stay with the Jaipur kids. It was like a palace! There was a bed, and past it there was a seating area with sea-foam-green rugs, marble tables encrusted with semi-precious stones and chairs embroidered with silken threads. On the furthest side was a cupboard.

'Well?' said Saif. 'What next?'

Ajay looked around, half expecting an alarm to go off. 'Do you think you can open the safe? It will probably be in the cupboard like it is in our hotel.'

'Why not?' said Saif as he walked across the room and opened the cupboard which, as Ajay had guessed, did have the safe in it. 'I am an apprentice engineer with an infinite amount of skills. What else am I going to do? Be part of the most important space programme in India?'

Ajay decided not to rise to the bait.

It did not take Saif long to open the safe.

'Ajay – over here!'

Inside was a slim file. Ajay flicked through – a brochure for The Four for 'Select Clients Only', and papers with two lists of names.

Ajay couldn't make any sense of it.

Why would anyone put a brochure and two lists of names in a safe?

'Ajay,' Saif's voice called behind him.

'Not now, Saif,' said Ajay. 'I'm thinking.'

'Ajay.'

'Not now.'

A low, heavy, metallic growling came from behind him.

Ajay stopped reading.

He slowly turned around, clutching the file tightly in his hand.

He had wondered why The Man in the Grey Suit had left everything unguarded.

The answer was that he hadn't.

Snarling at him and Saif, eyeball to eyeball, were two giant robotic dogs. Their mouths were filled with metal teeth that they bared at them, like daggers.

45

'How do I let you get me into this mess?' whimpered Saif, backing away from the robotic dogs so that he was standing behind Ajay.

Ajay would have replied – if he weren't fending off the two giant robot dogs with an upholstered chair. One bent its head, then snarled and gnashed at the chair's legs, causing them to crush and splinter between its chomping teeth. The red lights it had for eyes glowed like rubies.

Ajay gulped. 'Saif, we need a plan!'

'So now you ask me for my input?' said Saif from behind him, a note of grievance sounding over his fear. 'Am I never to be consulted until it is too late?'

The dogs came closer to Ajay, the metal ribs of their bodies heaving, their steel claws scratching the floor to shreds.

'Saif!' Ajay shouted, his hands grabbing a lamp, detaching the lampshade and waving it at the dogs.

'Oh, very well,' said Saif. 'We must have activated a sensor by the safe which woke the robot dogs up, but there will be a remote control that will override their programs. We just need to find it.'

One of the robot dogs leapt and grabbed the lamp out of Ajay's hand. Electricity sparked white-hot from the bulb, causing it to blaze with light. The smell of burning metal filled the room.

'How?'

'You need to distract the robot dogs, while I look for the remote control. They seem to have locked you in their sensors and they follow things that move – so keep running around. Give me about five minutes. Now go!'

Saif gave him a shove.

With nothing to protect him, Ajay ran to his

right, towards the bed, and the door out of the room just across it. In the mirror, he caught sight of the robot dogs as they paused, tilted their heads, looked at each other and then leapt after him.

Ajay jumped – running over the squashy mattress of the bed, losing his footing in the tangled sheets – and only just made it across. The robots leapt too, flaying the sheets and mattress to shreds, releasing a storm of white feathers everywhere.

'Go out of the room! I'll have more time that way,' shouted Saif impatiently.

Ajay raced out of the door and into the corridor. The robot dogs came chasing and barking after him.

'Oh look, Mum!' said a little toddler with red hair, standing in the open doorway of their room, their eyes big and round. 'They're making a film here!'

Ajay ran as fast as he could. The robot dogs chased him, their steel jaws snapping at his feet.

He shoved a dinner trolley in front of them and kept running.

He could hear it, and the bowls of sweet chum chums, drenched in syrup, slamming into them. It slowed them down – but it hadn't stopped them!

The lift was open. The poet, Dev, was sitting on a guest's suitcase still scribbling in his notebook.

'Quick! Close the door!' yelled Ajay, as he ran in.

'One second – just one more line,' said Dev, without looking up.

The dogs were closing in. Filled with terror, Ajay pressed the button and the doors closed – just in time to prevent the giant jaws from snapping him in two.

'Hey!' cried Dev looking up, his eyebrows pushed together, disgruntled.

'Sorry – an emergency!' gasped Ajay, adrenaline coursing through his veins. He looked through the ribs of the open lift and could see the metal dogs running down the stairs, their red eyes suddenly blue, as if they were scanning the blueprints of the hotel.

The doors of the lift screeched open, and Ajay ran out.

The dogs, who had been bounding down the stairs, took the last three steps in a single bound, their steel joints bending and flexing as they landed on the ground to the side of him.

'Live entertainment?' he heard one elderly guest wearing a tweed jacket in the reception say to another.

'Better than Las Vegas if you ask me!' said the guest's companion, busy taking photographs of the robots.

Ajay kept running.

The famous actor lifted his copy of *Julius Caesar*. 'I say – a brilliant visual representation: "Cry 'Havoc!' and let slip the dogs of war" and all that!'

Ajay had no time to respond. He was getting a stitch, and the robot dogs were right behind him! He stumbled in front of the table where the actress known for her martial arts films was drinking a cup of tea and eating a sweet of almond paste decorated with silver foil. 'I'm sorry,' Ajay puffed, close to collapse. 'Could you slow them down?' He stopped and pointed at the machines chasing after him.

The actress smiled, finished off the sip of tea and the sweetmeat, and turned to the robot dogs, throwing the saucer and plate with exquisite grace so that they caught them in their mouths like frisbees.

The robots yelped in surprise and stopped to drop them to the ground.

Ajay regained his breath. 'Thank you,' he said to her, running onwards.

He saw the NBA player next, who was leaning on a pillar of the hotel checking his phone. 'I'm sorry to disturb you, kind sir, but would you be able to help?'

The NBA player grinned down at Ajay from his great height. 'Sure. Why not?'

He put the phone in his pocket and moved forward, dribbling his basketball, racing round the robot dogs until they spun themselves dizzy, and came back to lean on the pillar again.

Ajay gave him a high-five, then turned and kept running until he came to the revolving doors.

They were jammed with luggage that was being loaded in on huge trollies. He was blocked. He whirled.

The robot dogs were in front of him, their teeth glinting in the light.

Ajay tugged at one of the tablecloths on the tables, whipping it so fast that all the plates and china clattered back in place. With sweat dripping into his eyes, he held the tablecloth to his side like a bullfighter.

One robot dog leapt. Ajay swirled, as the dog went through the cloth. Before Ajay could breathe, the other came tearing towards him.

Ajay threw the cloth! It landed over the dog who, snarling, ripped it into strips that floated down between them.

The robot dogs circled back in front, their jaws snapping.

Ajay stumbled. He had no energy left. There was nowhere to turn from here.

The dogs leant back on their hind legs, like coiled springs, ready to jump at him with their metal jaws wide. Their red eyes glittered.

Ajay held his arms out in front of him.

And all of a sudden they stopped, the red light in their eyes switched off and, deactivated, they collapsed comfortably to the ground.

Ajay gasped in relief.

Saif was standing behind them, waving the remote control.

46

Ajay and Saif were at the warehouse, where the Jaipur kids were letting them stay.

'And then,' said Saif, wolfing down a curry of chickpeas, simmered in a stew of melted-down tomatoes and chopped red onions, with colourful fried poppadoms, 'we gave lots of autographs, took the robot dogs back to the room and brought the file here.'

Saif had taken his time taking the dogs back to the room, Ajay remembered.

'And that's not all!' said Saif, bestowing them all with a look of exploding excitement. 'Look what I found in the cupboard!'

He stood up and pulled away a piece of cloth

with all the drama of a magician producing a rabbit.

Underneath the cloth was Saif's missing suit-case!

Jai pushed his hand through his hair. 'What I don't understand is why the CEO of a company with cutting-edge technology keeps everything on paper files?'

'Maybe it's because he doesn't trust computers?' Yasmin answered. She shrugged. 'But, Ajay – what's actually in the files?'

Ajay took out the brochure and opened it in front of the others, slightly embarrassed. After all, it did not seem a big enough prize for everything he and Saif had gone through! But then, as he flicked past the opening pages, his hands shook.

Inside were photos of deadly weapons.

Ajay struggled to breathe.

The Four was an international arms dealer, whose technology could be used to destroy anyone a client chose.

The brochure boasted of drones that could decide to kill people in swarms, AI machines that could lie in wait until activated by a specific target and robotic machine dogs – which made the ones that had chased him look like adorable puppies – that would only cause 'minimal' civilian casualties.

He stopped for a moment, feeling disembodied, unable to take in the full scope of what he was looking at. He wanted to fall on his knees.

How could anyone justify creating machines that could kill without mercy in this way? And then selling them on to the highest bidder – not even caring who would die from their use?

The others were staring at the brochure. Vinod and Jai in open-mouthed horror, Yasmin in utter fury and Saif in bewilderment. Laxmi was the only one not. She was looking at her hand with the missing finger.

'I can't look any more,' whispered Yasmin.

'It gets worse.' Haltingly, Ajay read the next section from the brochure out loud.

'*But for cases where weapons will draw too much attention – you need Spyware! The Four offers you the ability to select and control the people and organizations causing trouble in your life. We will trick those troublemakers into clicking on links that will instantly turn their mobile phones into video devices, and release details from their digital accounts. Using this private information, you will be able to force those trouble-makers into line! And you never need to worry about being held accountable as we guarantee to leave no trace of our work.'*

Ajay dropped the brochure, trying to stop his stomach from heaving. If this was what The Four could do now, what was it trying to do with the surveillance technology it was sending to space?

'The Four is evil!' Saif burst out, going closer to his suitcase as if it were a shield.

'So are the people buying and using its technology,' said Yasmin. Her voice could have frozen flames.

Only Jai looked unconvinced. 'I don't get it. How can surveillance technology be as dangerous as weapons?'

'Information is power,' said Vinod, his eyes dark. 'Mahesh had cameras installed in the kitchen of the old restaurant. The cook let slip that her brother was in jail and she couldn't afford to lose the job. Mahesh used the information he'd heard from the cameras to blackmail the cook into working for lower wages.'

Ajay nodded slowly. 'It's about control – just like the brochure says. Look at these two pages of names. The first is of politicians – including Mrs Shania – who support Mrs Surya having complete control over the Space Programme. There are sums of money next to their names—'

'Bribes?' interrupted Vinod.

'I guess so,' said Ajay. 'But there is also a second page. This time of politicians who have previously voted *against* Mrs Surya.'

Vinod took the paper from him, scanned it and turned pale. 'Ajay's right. And it's not just the names of politicians, but the names of human rights' lawyers – including Lata – union workers, Mrs Kajal, journalists. Mr Gupta's name is on this list!'

Comprehension showed on Yasmin's face. 'It's a list of people whose accounts are going to be illegally hacked.'

'Or have already been hacked,' interrupted Laxmi quietly.

'Look – our name is there!' said Saif, peering over Vinod's shoulder. Vinod gave the paper back to Ajay so that he could see. Saif was right. *The*

Mumbai Sun was listed – and next to it a note inked in pen – 'No digital footprint. Does *The Mumbai Sun* actually exist?'

'Of course we exist!' said Saif, outraged. 'Has The Man in the Grey Suit not read our work?'

Ajay bit his lip, feeling a wave of nausea. They had to stop The Four from sending its surveillance technology into space with the rocket to the moon! But the evidence was not yet complete – they still needed proof about who had committed the sabotage.

Yasmin was looking at the copy of the Minutes of the meeting that Mrs Surya had given him, that recorded what had been said between her and Mrs Kajal. She gave a soft cry of triumph. 'Ajay – the Minutes have a page missing. Look – it says page one and three, but no page two – and there's a tiny scrap of paper still attached to the staple. If we find page two, we might find out the truth!'

Yasmin was right!

And suddenly Ajay knew exactly what they and *The Mumbai Sun* needed to do next.

47

'**Y**ou really think this will work?' Jai asked Ajay.

'Don't worry, Jai! This is just plan A!' said Ajay. (He hoped Jai wouldn't ask if he had come up with a plan B.)

'What's your business?' said a security guard at the gate, in a stern voice.

Ajay coughed and tipped his fedora hat. 'We are here for the press conference this morning.'

The security guard looked up in surprise. 'All of you?'

Ajay looked behind him. Jai, holding the new cricket bat that Laxmi had made for him at the warehouse, nodded. Vinod smiled. Laxmi and

Yasmin tilted their heads. And Saif waved.

Ajay looked back at the guard. 'All of us,' he said firmly.

'But the press conference doesn't start for another two hours.'

Ajay leant forward. 'We are early,' he confirmed. 'But you see, we have travelled all the way from Mumbai this morning.'

The guard looked unimpressed. Before they could be turned back, Ajay explained. 'We are reporters from the very important newspaper, *The City Paper*. If you check your email, you'll see that our editor, Mr Gupta, has sent you photos, confirming our credentials.'

'Let me check,' said the guard, more impressed now that the name of one of the leading newspapers in India had been invoked! Ajay held his breath and crossed his fingers.

Had Mr Gupta got his telephone message in time?

The guard looked at them.

And nodded.

Ajay released his breath, turned to the others and winked. Mrs Surya might have revoked the security passes of *The Mumbai Sun*, but she hadn't counted on the help of its friends.

Phase one: complete!

48

Having got in, they made their way to Mrs Surya's office, flashing their press cards at anyone who challenged them. Saif and Laxmi got busy on the electronic lock and, with a beep and glitter of electronic lights, it opened.

Phase two was going to be a piece of cake!

They all entered – Jai, Laxmi and Yasmin, who hadn't seen it before, with a sharp intake of breath. High up, and in the blue light of morning, Ajay felt like he was standing in an iridescent bubble suspended in the air.

'Ajay, we don't have much time!' warned Yasmin. 'We have to get to the press conference!'

Ajay nodded, looking around. Mrs Surya had

guessed – from listening to their conversation with Anita? – that he might ask for the Minutes when she had called him up yesterday. He went behind her desk and tried to think like her. She had torn the second page out – and then what? There was no wastepaper bin near the desk, so either she had taken it with her or . . . dropped it back into her desk!

Ajay tried to open the drawer, but couldn't.

'Saif, Laxmi – can you open this?'

'I am an apprentice engineer!' said Saif, pride overcoming his fear of the glass floor. 'And Laxmi is a master jeweller. Of course we can!'

But it was soon clear that neither he nor Laxmi *could* unlock it!

'I'm sorry, Ajay,' said Laxmi. 'There is only one thing that will open this lock. The key.'

'How do we find a key in a space centre?' wondered Yasmin out loud.

'If it's even *in* the space centre,' said Jai, worried. 'Mrs Surya could have taken it with her.'

Ajay shook his head. He didn't think so. He remembered the key now – the gold, scrolled intricate barrel of it. Mrs Surya wasn't someone who would risk carrying the key around and it getting lost.

'It's in this room somewhere,' he said, more confidently than he felt. 'We need to search for it. Now!'

They sprang into action. On the tables, under the chairs, behind the single oil painting, across the floor – it did not take them long. Most of the office was glass – there was nowhere for the key to hide!

'We're doomed,' said Saif gloomily, his arms crossed, staring at the fish.

Ajay remembered Mrs Surya had been doing the same when she had called him – but what if actually she had not been watching the fish at all but had just taken out—

'Eureka!' he cried. 'The tank!'

The others looked at him in bewilderment.

'Do you need a nap, Ajay?' asked Saif, with sincere concern.

There was a flash of understanding in Vinod's eyes. He took the net at the side of the tank, lowering it carefully (so as not to disturb any of the fish) into the tank and drawing it back out.

Gleaming like buried treasure, in the net was the green-gold key!

Vinod gave it to Ajay with reverence, and they all crowded around Mrs Surya's desk.

Ajay closed his eyes for a second, then turned the key in the lock.

Click!

The others cheered in delight.

Ajay opened the drawer.

49

The first thing Ajay saw in the drawer of Mrs Surya's desk was the second page of the Minutes. He had guessed right! She had dropped it in there quickly. There was a little tear in the left-hand corner, where it had been torn from the staple attaching it to the rest.

He picked it up and read it.

Then he turned to Jai, Vinod, Saif, Yasmin and Laxmi, who were staring at him in silence.

'We've got it,' he said quietly. 'Proof.'

They linked hands in a moment of support, and relief, and exhilaration.

'What does it say?' asked Saif tremulously.

Ajay started by pointing to the top of the page.

'The Minutes record what happened at this part of the meeting. Mrs Surya was furious at Mrs Kajal for stopping her from building factories in space.'

'Stopping her? How?' asked Jai, scratching his head as he looked at the sheet of paper. 'Mrs Surya owns WECU!'

Ajay nodded. 'But the politicians put Mrs Kajal in charge of overseeing the Programme. Mrs Surya couldn't do anything without Mrs Kajal agreeing—'

'—which is why she needed Mrs Kajal to be replaced by The Four, who *would* support the factories,' whispered Yasmin, with sudden understanding. 'Mrs Shania and Mr Jalebi had already – if we're right about the first page of names – been bribed to agree to Mrs Kajal's replacement. If The Four won the race for the meteorite, the rest of the politicians would too. They couldn't disagree! That's what all the drones were for – so The Four could, in a so-called fair race, covered by every newspaper in the country, prove their technical skills were the best in India!'

'But we won instead.' Ajay nodded in satisfaction at their success. 'So Mrs Surya got The Four to hack into Mrs Kajal's accounts to find a way to blackmail her. But *that* didn't work because Mrs Kajal found out about the hacking. Look – it says here that she brought the evidence for Mrs Surya to see at the meeting.'

'I thought that The Four said that their hacking was untraceable?' interrupted Jai, tapping the desk.

Laxmi's green eyes glittered. 'The Four under-estimated her, despite all her achievements. Mrs Kajal was Chief Scientist of the Space Programme. Did they really think she wouldn't notice?'

'She put The Four's business at risk. Their clients would know that their hacking could be traced. No wonder they and Mrs Surya needed to get rid of her,' mused Yasmin.

'And Mrs Surya *did* have another plan in place,' said Ajay. 'Framing Mrs Kajal for sabotage and laying the clues for us to discover it. But Mrs Kajal was too thorough,' said Ajay, scanning down the document. 'She found out that there was no camera recording of the first sabotage attempt and so investigated further and discov-ered that Mrs Surya had tampered with the security footage. The cover-up literally led to the crime! It says here that in the meeting, Mrs Kajal gave Mrs Surya twenty-four hours to turn herself in.'

'A mistake,' said Vinod quietly.

Ajay felt sad. 'She thought Mrs Surya was like her. She thought that Mrs Surya would take the chance to do the honourable thing.'

'She underestimated Mrs Surya's ruthlessness,' said Laxmi bluntly. 'She shouldn't have. She should have seen the endgame.' Ajay wondered for a moment at the dark bitterness underneath Laxmi's words.

'The ultimatum was why Mrs Surya got careless though,' said Yasmin. 'She only had twenty-four hours to commit the final acts of sabotage *and* make sure that we found them. So she put explosives on the rocket and cut the seat belt on the pod – quick to do and obvious to find . . .'

They looked at each other. Ajay felt ashamed at how quickly they had assumed Mrs Kajal's guilt.

'There's still not enough evidence,' Saif whispered from behind them.

They turned. Saif was shaking. His face was frozen.

And Ajay remembered that of all of them, Saif had believed in Mrs Surya the most and had been the most hurt at the revelations in the file of The Four.

'No, but this might be,' said Ajay as gently as he could. Using a tissue so as not to disturb any prints, he showed them a small dagger with a serrated edge. Mrs Surya's name was engraved on the worn handle in liquid silver. 'The slashes on the seat belt in the capsule: I think they were made with this.'

As the others looked at it, Ajay tried to keep his balance. The terror of the spinning capsule and those moments when he had thought he would not survive still had him in their grip.

Mrs Surya must have been cutting the seat belt as they entered the astronaut training facility! She had tried to kill him to give herself time to plant the evidence in Mrs Kajal's desk, knowing that the broken seat belt and explosive device would easily be found before it could do any real damage to the Space Programme.

Ajay felt weak. He had thought she was a friend. How could he have been so wrong? Every step of this had been planned. Mrs Surya had even used her knowledge that he could not swim. She had guessed that once he got to the vast training area he would search the pod first rather than the pool, and so had chosen it as the place to sabotage.

Yasmin and Vinod moved to stand closer to him, as if sensing that he needed them.

'It's not your fault, Ajay,' said Yasmin in a low voice. 'We all wanted to believe in her.'

'There's still more here,' said Jai, taking out a cube and a sheaf of papers from the drawer. His face went pale; his whole body went rigid.

'What is it, Jai?' asked Vinod.

'Proof that Mrs Surya paid The Four to hack anyone opposed to her.'

Ajay relaxed. 'But that's evidence—'

'I've not finished,' Jai said, cutting in. 'There's also a Partnership Agreement between Mrs Surya and The Four. Ajay – it's worse than we ever imagined. The surveillance technology The Four wants to send into space with Mrs Surya's rocket will allow The Four to spy on every single person in India! The Four won't need people to click on links. Its spyware will watch us and hack everything we do automatically by satellite. The Four will then sell the information they collect to the highest bidder. And in return—'

'And in return,' said Mrs Surya's voice from the doorway, 'The Four – and its spyware – will support me in making my colonies in space become reality. Nothing in the future – not even *The Mumbai Sun* – will stop the new factories I have planned!'

They whirled.

There in the doorway were Mrs Surya and The Man in the Grey Suit, five towering security guards—

And the two snarling robot dogs.

50

Ajay, looking at Mrs Surya with new eyes, shuddered. He had once thought that she was magical. But now he understood that the magic hadn't come from her at all – it was he who had been projecting it on to her.

Mrs Surya stepped in and, with a glancing sweep, took everything in. She smiled sadly. 'Ajay, I so wish you had taken me up on my offer. So much unpleasantness could have been avoided.'

Unpleasantness? She had tried to kill him!

As if she had heard his thoughts, Mrs Surya shook her head. 'Everyone is expendable, Ajay. I would have felt – sorrow – at your death, but I had to be rational. I could not risk you seeing me before I had managed to plant the evidence inside Mrs Kajal's desk. And I had to make the calculation that even with you gone I would still achieve my aim. Your friends would have stopped at nothing to take revenge on Mrs Kajal when I convinced them she had killed you.'

Ajay's fury almost blinded him.

But it was Saif who stepped forward, straightening his shirt awkwardly as he spoke to her.

'I am an apprentice engineer who wanted to work on a space rocket,' he said with humbling dignity. 'I did not want to be part of a programme that will spy on my friends and people across India so that they can be blackmailed.'

Ajay bit his lip, his heart aching for him.

Mrs Surya laughed as she looked at Saif.

'Work on a space rocket? You? You call yourself an apprentice engineer, but do you know what I found when I hacked into telephone records of the engineers you work with in Mumbai?'

Saif became still, his eyes filled with sudden yearning and hope.

Mrs Surya waited, letting the moment play out.

'Don't you dare,' whispered Laxmi, her breath jagged.

And, in sudden panic, Ajay realized that Laxmi was a step ahead and that the rest of the team had underestimated Mrs Surya again.

'They *laugh* at you, Saif!' Mrs Surya's voice was filled with amusement. 'They mock you. They wish you wouldn't always hang around. And as for being an apprentice engineer? They certainly don't think of you as that. They consider you more of a – what was the word in the message again? – ah, yes. "A pest".'

Saif's face, soft with eagerness, became still.

It took a moment for her words to hit.

And when they did, Ajay saw his face crumble.

Saif dropped his head.

'Of course, they know more than me,' Saif said quietly. He wiped his eyes. 'And I should have realized that I was disturbing them. I shouldn't really . . .'

Jai put his arm around Saif's shoulder, in a quiet act of reassurance. Vinod stood in front of the two of them with his saucepan held as a barrier, as if by that alone he could deflect Mrs

Surya's words.

Laxmi and Yasmin came together in front of Vinod – Yasmin quivering with an anger that, if unleashed, would set not just the room but the whole of Jaipur on fire; Laxmi's leaf-green eyes ice-cold with hate.

Mrs Surya was unaffected. She smiled and looked at Ajay.

And he could read her thoughts as clearly as if she had written them.

No one ever says no to me without paying a price.

She had followed through on her threat, in the cruellest way that she could.

By making him watch his friend suffer.

51

Mrs Surya looked at her watch. 'Well, as fun as this has been, we have a press conference to get to.'

'You won't get away with this,' said Ajay, hearing the tinkling hollowness of the words as he said them.

Mrs Surya laughed in genuine amusement. 'Of course I will, and I will be worshipped for it.'

And Ajay suddenly, aware of all her shimmering power to manipulate people, didn't doubt it.

The Man in the Grey Suit stepped forward, and with him the two robot dogs, twisting their enormous heads, their ruby-red eyes burning hot and dark as they spied Ajay and his friends. There was something different about them – a new program? Ajay was shaken – if they had looked like dangerous machines before, now they looked like hellhounds.

'The robots can stay inside the room and make sure that Ajay and his friends don't leave,' said Mrs Surya to The Man in the Grey Suit. 'We'll decide what to do with them after the press conference, once all the journalists are gone. Oh, and make sure that you keep the remote with you this time?'

The Man in the Grey Suit lifted his head, a flicker in his eyes showing that the barb had not gone unnoticed.

Ajay shivered, and for a brief moment wondered if Mrs Surya knew what she was doing in provoking him.

'What about us?' said the guards.

Mrs Surya turned to them with a raised eyebrow. 'I think weapons that have crushed tanks on battlefields will suffice to keep them in check, don't you? You come with us.'

She turned and gave Ajay one final, sweeping, triumphant glance, but her voice when she spoke seemed to hold a genuine note of regret.

'You really should have taken me up on my offer, Ajay. Together we could have changed the world.'

And then she turned and left with the guards.

Ajay ran towards the door. If he could just get to the press conference—

The Man in the Grey Suit turned from the door, his eyes as blue as mist.

He caught Ajay by the front of his shirt and slammed him into the wall.

Ajay gasped with the impact.

For a moment, he wondered if his spine had shattered.

The Man in the Grey Suit smiled, savouring the moment. Then he turned and left, blotting out the light from the corridor, before anyone else had time to react.

The door shut behind him.

The pain made Ajay's eyes swim.

Gripping on to the edge of the seat nearby, Ajay forced himself up and, through the agony, ran towards the door – he had to get the story out! He had to find a way to free Mrs Kajal and to stop the technology created by The Four being sent to space with the rocket.

He was stopped by the dagger-like teeth of the dogs coming towards him.

There was no way to get out.

They were trapped.

And Mrs Surya and The Man in the Grey Suit had won.

52

The dogs circled in front of Ajay, the metal joints of their bodies flexing, their metal teeth snapping and their metal claws scratching.

'Ajay, get back!' called Jai, fear in his voice.

Ajay backed away. No one could get past these robot dogs, and this time there was nowhere for him to run.

And then, from the corner of his eye, Ajay saw Saif walking towards the dogs.

'Saif! No!' cried Yasmin, realizing too late what Saif was doing.

He was walking towards the dogs with his shoulders bowed – as if still carrying the wounds of Mrs Surya's words.

'Saif, stop!' Ajay called out in genuine terror. The robot dogs moved away from Ajay, stalking Saif, not letting him out of their sight.

Tensing its hind legs, one leapt.

Ajay ran. He saw, as if in slow motion, Jai, Vinod, Yasmin and Laxmi running to put themselves between Saif and the robot dog too.

But none of them would get there in time.

'Saif!' Ajay sobbed.

Saif looked up, his face shining, as if he was unaware of the danger he was in from the dog and its extended metal-edged claws.

And then, just as Ajay was sure it was going to be all too late, Saif smiled. 'Laika!'

The robot dog landed just centimetres in front of him – and nuzzled his hand!

Ajay stopped, feeling as if he had crashed into an invisible wall. His heart hammered in his chest.

What was going on?

The other dog followed Laika's lead.

Ajay saw Jai trip over in shock at the way the robot dogs were jumping playfully around Saif as if they were old friends. 'Saif?' he said, looking at a complete loss.

Saif was petting Laika. Then he looked up, and Ajay felt relief wash over him.

The wounds inflicted on Saif by Mrs Surya's words had healed.

'When we were at the hotel and I took the robot dogs back up to the room, I thought I would make some modifications,' said Saif.

'Modifications?' Ajay echoed.

Saif nodded firmly. 'I called the leader of the pack Laika. She's named after the dog that was sent to die in space on Sputnik II – a stray who, just like us, lived on the streets.' He paused, then spoke again. 'It is very difficult for most people to program in name recognition. But whatever Mrs Surya, and even the other engineers, think,' he took a deep breath, 'I am an—'

'Apprentice engineer!' said everyone at once.

Saif looked at them in surprise. And nodded.

The others fell on top of him, hugging him and ruffling his hair. Saif looked pleased and embarrassed, both at once.

'What are we going to do next, Ajay?' said Yasmin eventually. 'The press conference is going to start soon.'

Ajay looked around at his friends and lifted his head.

They did not have long.

He took a deep breath.

'What we came here to do.'

Ajay took out Mr Gupta's notebook and pen. He remembered all that they had done to get there – the race for the meteorite, the battle of the drones, the sabotage attempt – and squared his shoulders.

If Mrs Surya and The Man in the Grey Suit wanted a battle, they were going to get one.

'We're going to bring out the next issue of *The Mumbai Sun*.'

53

The press conference had started. As Ajay threaded his way through the crowd, he saw Mrs Surya standing on the podium with The Man in the Grey Suit. In front of them, on a crystal stand, was an intricate piece of machinery made of glass and silver.

Mrs Surya glittered from top to toe in a lace sari that was encrusted with diamonds and looked like clouds of the Milky Way. She was smiling at the audience, who had come from every part of the globe and were now standing in hushed silence. Their eyes reflected the sparkle around them, as if aware of how significant the occasion was.

Mrs Surya opened her arms.

'We have come together, the day before the launch, not only to celebrate a new day for space travel, but a new era! This is the final piece of the engine that we will set into the rocket today.'

There was a burst of applause.

Mrs Surya caught it like a wave, and her eyes lit with excitement. The lamps shone down on her, and she looked like a figure spun from light.

The crowd stilled.

'People think that billionaires across the world, like myself, are only interested in escaping Earth and its problems. My vision is greater than that. Climate change is wrecking our world. I have a solution!'

The audience gasped. Every one of them, from every country in the world, had felt in one form or another the ravages of the extreme weather – the burning days, the cities under flood and on fire, the crops and livestock that had perished. If Mrs Surya had a solution, they looked ready to listen!

Mrs Surya's voice wove around them like music. 'As you know, the WECU corporation owns factories across the globe. With the willing support of politicians, I will move them into space so that they no longer pollute our world. No longer bogged down with laws and human rights, these factories will be a blueprint for oligarchs everywhere.'

The crowd applauded.

'And they are just the beginning of my plans for space and for Earth.'

More applause. Mrs Surya basked in it for a moment, then returned to business.

'So, on the advent of our rocket's journey to the moon, I ask you to raise a toast – to my dream – to *our* collective dream – of colonizing and conquering space and creating a new society for all!'

The crowd lifted their hands, ready to clap.

Ajay burst through and stood at the front.

'Except what you are describing is not a dream at all,' said Ajay. 'It's a nightmare, dripping with blood and violence, and it needs to be stopped!'

54

Mrs Surya and The Man in the Grey Suit looked at Ajay in shock.

'What are you doing here?' hissed Mrs Surya, as he climbed the podium.

Ajay looked at them with contempt. 'What do you think? Telling the truth.' He took a deep breath and turned to the crowd. 'I am Ajay, editor of *The Mumbai Sun*. You have heard from Mrs Surya about her dream – but now you will hear about its cost.'

'You're wasting your breath,' Mrs Surya said to him softly. 'A crowd like this wants a spectacle. I can write my message across skies. What can *The Mumbai Sun* do without a printer?'

Ajay smiled.

Saif stepped forward from the crowd, a small figure against the hundreds of people behind him, and hit a button.

The dark glass walls on all four sides suddenly changed colour.

They changed colour to bright, glowing faluda pink – and on them, shining in towering letters, was the latest edition of *The Mumbai Sun*!

Saif waved and bowed at the crowd to a burst of applause.

'Saif is *The Mumbai Sun*'s Apprentice Engineer,' Ajay answered, equally softly. 'We can do a lot.'

And for the first time since he had known her Mrs Surya looked afraid.

Ajay walked to the mic and, once the crowd became still, said, 'Let me begin.'

Armed with the text and moving images that Yasmin and Laxmi had animated on screen, Ajay began to speak. He told the crowd of how the meteorite race had been planned so that The Man in the Grey Suit would win and The Four would be put forward as a partner of the Space Programme to replace Mrs Kajal. He described how Mrs Surya had planned the sabotage, using *The Mumbai Sun* and its reputation for uncovering corruption to give legitimacy to its discovery. He described how, to get complete control, she had planted the evidence against Mrs Kajal (trying to kill him in the process) so that Mrs Kajal would be removed from the Space Programme.

'This is a fabrication!' Mrs Surya called out.

'Guards! Get him out of here.'

The guards moved forward, but Vinod and Jai stepped out with the two robot dogs, who looked at the guards with their red, glowing eyes.

The guards stepped back.

On screen came details from The Four's brochure. As images of their weapons, and the deaths they could cause, burnt on the screen, the crowd became silent in horror. It was one thing to hear of weapons in theory – but to see the horrors they could unleash was clearly, from their reactions, another. And then, Ajay showed them and explained the list of names with sums next to them, together with the list of names of people whose accounts had been hacked to know their every move and find a way to get them to support Mrs Surya's programme of factories in space. The crowd recoiled.

'It's a lie!' said Mrs Surya, backing away. 'Fake news!'

'Actually, it's not,' said a gravelly voice from the crowd.

'Mr Gupta!' said Ajay, joyful at seeing his old friend in his crumpled suit and worn-out shoes.

'Sorry I'm late, Ajay,' said Mr Gupta. 'It took some time gathering the evidence you asked for.'

'That's OK, Mr Gupta! I'm glad you came!' said Ajay. Then, in case he forgot later, added, 'And thank you for lending me your notebook and pen!'

Mr Gupta nodded gruffly and turned to the crowd, his presence commanding. 'I am the editor of *The City Paper*. As one of the names on the list, I had software engineers do a scan on my phone. They found malware on it. The other people on the list have been informed. They too have found proof that their personal details have been hacked.'

'That's impossible. The Four said that the hacking was undetectable!' said Mrs Surya, then turned, her eyes wide, her brow drawn with sweat, as she suddenly seemed to realize that her own words confirmed her guilt.

'Not if you know what you are looking for,' said Mrs Kajal coolly, her cobalt-blue sari catching the light as she, Anita and Lata, Ajay's lawyer friend from Mumbai, stepped forward. Ajay waved to Lata in greeting and she waved back. Mrs Kajal continued, 'And I have set out the specifications of the code in the public domain. Now anyone in the world will be able to check if their personal details have been hacked.' She turned to The Man in the Grey Suit. 'I suspect you might soon be receiving a lot of calls.'

The Man in the Grey Suit looked as if he had eaten a plate of chillies that were too hot for him.

Ajay watched him carefully. Had Mrs Surya been in control, or had she been used? Ajay was no longer sure. The Man in the Grey Suit and his organization, The Four, might have worked in the shadows, but they had played political games – profiting from war, surveillance and torture – all over the world.

The foreign journalists started looking at their phones as they began to ring, presumably with calls from people in their own countries who had been hacked by The Four!

'How did you get out?' said Mrs Surya to Mrs Kajal, staring at her as if she were a ghost.

Mrs Kajal looked Mrs Surya directly in the

eye, strain showing in the way she held herself, and Ajay suddenly wondered what it had been like for her to be silenced in a prison cell, knowing that she was innocent, whilst the person who had framed her was being hailed as a saviour. 'Once Ajay sent me and my lawyer, Lata, the information from the files, the charges against me were dropped.'

Mrs Surya looked trapped.

Ajay turned as the final page of *The Mumbai Sun* was shown on screen. 'The technology that The Four and Mrs Surya wanted to send into space was spyware.'

It was time for the last line of the article: 'Mrs Surya intended to hack the private information of every single person in India. People like us.'

He gave a signal.

Saif pressed a button.

The screens went dark, and then turned into giant silvery mirrors. The crowd saw itself in them, and their eyes looked shocked. Ajay could see the message – that next time, it could be *them* – hit home.

Ajay looked around, pleased at their reaction

to his theatrical finish.

Sometimes you needed to be a bit over the top to sell the news!

55

As the police came forward from the crowd, Mrs Surya grabbed the mic.

Surely she knew that the game was over?

But Mrs Surya glittered in the light, and Ajay remembered that he should not underestimate her. She could hypnotize a snake-charmer.

She spoke to the crowd, sounding reasonable and rational. 'Wait! Listen! I agree my methods might have been wrong, but was my aim?'

The crowd looked up to her.

'Don't you want to be rich?' Her voice was as soft and unthreatening as milk. 'It is important not to see things as black and white. We Explore to Commercialize the Universe. Those factories that I wished to build in space, the ones that Mrs Kajal is against and that I have had to go to such lengths to try to bring about – they'd be producing goods for *you*. And because our factories would be operating at next to no cost, goods would be cheaper than you have ever been able to buy them before. Don't you want that?'

Some in the crowd wavered.

There was a moment of silence, and suddenly Ajay was afraid that some people in the crowd would once again, in this last moment, fall for her argument.

He was about to speak when Laxmi's voice, full of pain, broke the spell.

'Except there's always a cost, even if you choose not to see it.' Laxmi stepped forward, her leaf-green eyes dark with knowledge that could only have been gained from experience. Yasmin was by her side. 'Many of you are wearing gold necklaces – some of them ones that I have made. You bought them from WECU factories. You should know that there was a cost to them. You might not have paid, but workers – like me – did.' The bitterness in her voice scraped the air.

Ajay took a harsh breath. There was no choice. The crowd had to see Mrs Surya's dream for what it was. They had to see what Mrs Kajal and *The Mumbai Sun* had been fighting against.

Ajay threw the cube that Jai had found in Mrs Surya's desk on stage. Holograms flooded the space above them, flickering with a cold blue light. 'Mrs Surya wants factories in space, but they are modelled on the very worst on Earth,' said Ajay, his voice low. 'Look.'

And the crowd looked and saw people toiling in conditions that not a single person in the crowd could bear to think about, never mind suffer themselves, for a second.

One by one each member of the crowd bowed their heads in a public rejection of Mrs Surya and her dream. A few took off their gold necklaces.

They had finally seen the horrific conditions that they had previously – determinedly – looked away from.

And had, at last, understood.

Police came on to the stage. 'You are under arrest,' they said to Mrs Surya and The Man in the Grey Suit.

Mrs Surya looked at them in disbelief. 'You dare?'

Lata spoke then, the light gleaming on her nut-brown hair. 'They do, but don't worry,' she added seriously, 'I will make sure that you both have all your rights.'

The police gathered to escort Mrs Surya and The Man in the Grey Suit down from the podium.

Mrs Surya turned and snarled. 'If I can't realize my dream of space, no one else will either.'

Ajay watched, and knew it was too late to stop her.

She pushed the crystal stand, and the intricate machinery on it smashed. The last part of the rocket! Ajay stood, stunned. Without it, the rocket mission was doomed.

Mrs Surya looked at them. And in her eyes was a twisted coil of triumph. 'You've failed,' she hissed.

Mrs Kajal stepped forward. 'That's where you're wrong,' she said simply.

Mrs Surya was taken away.

Mrs Kajal closed her eyes for a moment. Then, opening them, she turned calmly to the piece of machinery. 'Call the engineers. Let's get to work.' She tilted her head as she looked at the broken machinery in front of her, as if taking it apart and putting it together with her mind. Ajay watched her in awe. He finally understood her. She might be the least arrogant person he had ever met – but she was also the most able!

Mrs Kajal turned. 'Saif, Laxmi – we could use your skills to help to mend this in time. Will you help?' she said smiling.

Laxmi's eyes lost all their bitterness and filled with pride.

Saif looked at the others, who nodded encouragingly at him. Equal parts joy that Mrs Kajal had asked him for help, and terror that Mrs Kajal might change her mind, seemed to flash across his face. Then he ran to help her with the machine as fast as his legs could carry him.

Ajay's heart felt warm. Saif had got his dream. He would work on a rocket that would fly to the moon!

56

It was dawn. The sky was a soft rosy pink. Ajay, Vinod, Yasmin, Jai, Laxmi and Saif were sitting together on a blanket on the roof of the WECU building. Mrs Kajal had offered them the command centre, but Ajay had wanted to give *The Mumbai Sun* readers a different perspective. The others had agreed.

The rocket shimmered in the distance, ready for its journey.

Vinod, having smuggled Anita a special masala chapati wrap to eat on the spacecraft, had made them an early morning breakfast. To their delight, he set out plates of fried paratha with sweet raw mango chutney, and cups of steaming chai, flavoured with smoky cinnamon and crushed cardamom.

Ajay, touched by Vinod's kindness, held a cup of chai in his chilled hands to warm them. In his mind's eye, he saw people across India waiting too. There would be kids in the slum, awake and sitting by blue open flames, sketching rockets in charcoal on the ground. There would be adults in temporary makeshift homes standing at the edges of their single rooms with chipped cups of coffee growing cold in their hands. And there would be elderly people switching on digital screens, their faces luminous with light-shot memories of the first moon landing they had seen on crackly black-and-white television sets.

Ajay looked around him. Laxmi and Saif had stayed up all night helping Mrs Kajal and were now sitting next to each other. Saif was quiet, as though to say anything would jinx the launch, holding a phone that Mrs Kajal had given him so tightly that his knuckles shone. Laxmi looked exhausted but radiant, the single silver bracelet on her wrist turning rose gold in the sun's light.

Jai and Vinod were whiling away the time:

Vinod counting down, whilst Jai repeatedly bounced a cricket ball on his bat. It caught the light of the sun like a red fireball.

Yasmin was sitting next to him, the proud bones of her face illuminated in the sun's light. Her emerald eyes were focused on the rocket in front of them.

'You're worried about Anita?' Ajay said softly.

Yasmin nodded. 'If anything goes wrong with the launch . . .'

Ajay shook his head. 'It won't.'

But against the light and shining promise of the day was also the knowledge of what had happened to Kalpana Chawla – the first Indian woman astronaut, whose extraordinary life still inspired them all and whose death had been a tragedy. On her second mission she had been one of seven crew members who had died in the Space Shuttle Columbia disaster when the spacecraft disintegrated during re-entry.

'Why do you want to be an astronaut when it's so dangerous and leave me, Yasmin?' Ajay burst out, no longer able to keep the words inside. 'I thought you wanted to be an illustrator for *The*

Mumbai Sun?'

Yasmin didn't answer for a long time, her eyes still gazing outward.

Ajay felt afraid.

Then she spoke.

'I know it's dangerous to be an astronaut. Anita told me space flight can affect your bones, your heart – even your eyes.' She trembled, and Ajay knew what that meant to Yasmin who saw the world in lines and colours. 'But I can't help it. I want to see the universe – like a fish trapped in a bowl that wants to see the ocean. I want to see it for myself and find a way to draw it!'

She turned to look at Ajay. Her eyes sparkled. 'And it's not about leaving you – it's about me, and what I want. But if I do leave, Ajay, we'll always be a part of each other.' She shrugged and said matter-of-factly, as if the words conveyed it all, 'We're friends.'

Ajay looked away, trying to hide the feelings in his heart.

Just because his mother had left him, didn't mean others would too.

And if they did leave, he would still be OK.

As would they.

He breathed out and chose not to be afraid.

Saif was looking at his phone. It beeped. He shot up and waved it. 'It's time.'

57

Ten.

Ajay standing with Jai, Yasmin, Saif, Laxmi and Vinod.

Nine.

A rumble of rocket engines.

Eight.

Clouds of white smoke.

Seven.

Gold sparks.

Six.

Hands linking together.

Five.

A burst of orange fire.

Four.

Gold jets.

Three.

Engines pivoting.

Two.

Flames pouring.

One.

Torrents – waterfalls – of fire rolling.

58

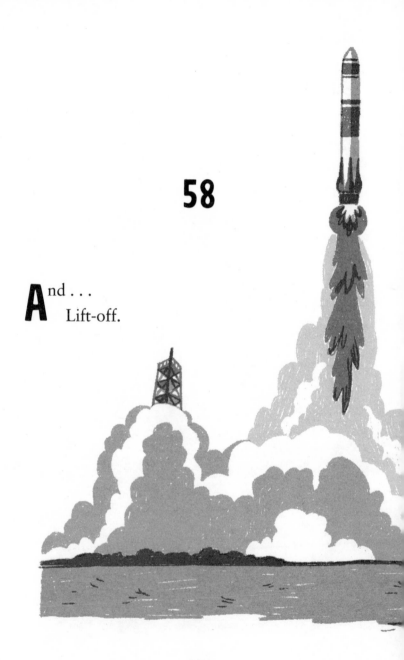

And . . .
   Lift-off.

59

Ajay watched as the rocket powered into the air, lifted up by rolling jets of flames and smoke.

What could he say in *The Mumbai Sun* that would convey the feeling of light and magic and joy and the heart-stopping wonder of it? The feeling that time itself had stopped?

And then he had it. A fragment of a line that Niresh had once read to him.

'We are such things as dreams are made on.'

60

As Ajay ran through the streets of Mumbai, his heart was beating fast in his chest.

Immediately after the rocket launch, three things had happened. Mrs Kajal had been put in charge of the newly named Rainbow Phoenix Space Programme. Ajay and the others had said goodbye to Laxmi and the Jaipur kids (who, as soon as Laxmi's work on the space rocket became known, had enough orders for jewellery to keep them in business for a year). And Saif had improved the engines of the rickshaws of Rikesh the Rickshaw driver's friends, cousins and relatives, so that the whole of Jaipur now ran twice as fast!

Mr Gupta had bought the story from *The Mumbai Sun* to distribute (with their names still on the byline and a percentage of each copy sold!) through *The City Paper*.

'I can't pay you much,' he said. 'People are still unwilling to pay what they can have for free – but,' and his eyes crinkled, 'it will be enough for a secondhand printing press, a pen and a notebook!' It had been time for Ajay to return to Mumbai and get his mother's pen back.

Ajay ran into Mr Soni's shop. The bell clanged behind him.

'I've got the money!' he shouted.

Mr Soni looked at him, his watch glinting in the light. 'You are meant to come through the back door.'

Ajay was too excited to worry about that. 'I have the money for my mother's pen.' He put the cash on the table. 'Can I have it now?'

Mr Soni slowly picked up the notes and counted them, one by one.

Ajay waited, tremulous with excitement. He imagined the first story he would write when he got it back!

'I'm sorry, but this is not enough.'

Ajay looked at him blankly.

'Of course it is enough. It is the sum I paid.'

Mr Soni looked at him from above. 'It is, but you need to pay four times as much. You see, there is the interest. You can see that you agreed to it here.' Mr Soni showed him the note, with barely hidden satisfaction.

Ajay froze. The sum was larger than anything his worst nightmares could conjure.

'I don't have it,' Ajay whispered.

'Then I am afraid that it will not be possible to get your mother's pen back.'

'I can come back with the money,' said Ajay desperately. 'I'll find a way to get it.'

Mr Soni looked at him with relish. 'It will – unfortunately – be too late. You see, I have already secured a buyer in Switzerland to buy the pen. They will officially own it when the clock runs out, which is in the next five minutes.'

Ajay wanted to shout, to cry, to do anything that would convince Mr Soni to give him his mother's pen back.

The bell above the door rang behind them.

Mr Soni looked up, all smiles, which disappeared the moment he saw who it was.

'The back door only, please,' he said sharply.

'We're here to get Ajay's pen,' Ajay heard Yasmin's voice say.

Ajay whirled. Saif, Vinod, Yasmin and Jai were standing there breathless, looking as if they had run all the way.

'What are you doing here?' said Ajay.

'What do you think?' said Yasmin, shaking her head. 'Did you really think you had fooled us with that story of keeping your mother's pen safe with Mr Sandhu? We knew you wouldn't ever part with it.'

'And you suddenly had enough money for the tickets—' said Saif.

'And then you rushed off when we arrived in Mumbai,' said Vinod.

'And we followed you!' said Jai. 'Or tried to – we lost you for a bit, but now we've found you.'

Ajay looked at them all.

Yasmin walked to Mr Soni. 'Give me the slip,' she said. When Mr Soni looked as if he was about to argue, she said, 'Now. Unless you want everyone in the slum to know that you cheat?'

Mr Soni showed her the sum. Yasmin's eyes widened, but she brought out the money.

Ajay looked at her in shock. 'Yasmin – that's the money for the printer.'

'It's OK, Ajay. We'll find another way,' said Jai.

Ajay knew he should argue, but he couldn't. All he could do was stand and wait, as Mr Soni brought out his mother's pen.

The others waited in reverent silence as Ajay took it from him. His heart swelled as he saw its black barrel and gold nib. His mother's pen. It was back, safe and sound.

He turned to the others and held it in the air.

And with it came a plan of what to do next!

61

Ajay looked around joyfully at the area in front of the station. Mr Gupta and Mrs Kajal had made some calls and got permission for the team from *The Mumbai Sun* to have a special one-day, space-themed fundraising event!

People were thronging the stalls. They were buying space-themed food: sweet, doughy, moon-shaped ghugara; floury chapatti wraps just like the one the astronaut Anita ate in space on her way to the moon; and rocket-shaped, rainbow-bright kulfi desserts! They were buying drawings of the rocket and portraits of Anita by Yasmin. They were listening to a special lecture by Saif, Apprentice Engineer, on a podium. And they were watching the end of a one-day friendly cricket match between the team from the slums and the team from Calcutta.

As the day drew to a close, the team from *The Mumbai Sun* gathered together and counted up the money.

'How did the cricket match go?' Ajay asked Jai.

Jai smiled, his golden eyes bright. 'We lost – just! But we've scheduled in more for next month.'

Ajay looked at him, relieved.

Jai caught the look and laughed out loud. 'Don't worry, Ajay. I'm fine.'

And Ajay saw that he really was. Jai knew his own worth now.

Vinod had finished counting.

'Well?' asked Saif. 'Don't keep us waiting. I am very busy at the moment. I have promised to sign at least a hundred autographs.'

Vinod took a deep breath.

'It's enough,' he said quietly. And then, in case they had not understood, said, 'It's enough to buy a printing press.'

For a moment, they looked at each other in

shock. Then they cheered. From the corner of his eye, Ajay thought he saw a shooting star (or perhaps Anita's rocket!) trailing across the sky.

A very good omen for the very next (soon to be print!) edition of their paper: *The Mumbai Sun*!

ACKNOWLEDGEMENTS

To Lou Kuenzler and the City Lit workshop and class members who have taught, helped and encouraged throughout – thank you for everything. The reality is that this book could only have been written with you there. Thanks to Cath, Jo, Hannah and Beth for your time.

To my friends and family.

To Mrs Woods and in memory of Mrs Sandy Millar. To Keith, Kieran, Melanie, the 'Wombats', the Ruffles, 7-10L, Tomoko San, Sunagawa San and family, the basketball and cricket players, and my friends in Japan, Canada and Sydney.

To Barry Cunningham and everyone at Chicken House for championing this book and putting so much of your time, experience and expertise into it – and for continuing to make dreams come true.

And finally, as always, to the students I have taught – wherever you are I wish you tenderness and joy.

Ajeet Prabhu/Sidney Sarpong

Varsha Shah always dreamt of being a writer. After studying Law at Cambridge University, she worked as a solicitor and has written articles for various publications. She is now an English teacher, and has taught English as a foreign language in both Japan and Canada. She loves travelling and is completely obsessed with basketball.

BEETLE BOY by M. G. LEONARD

Darkus can't believe his eyes when a huge insect drops out of the trouser leg of his horrible new neighbour. It's a giant beetle – and it seems to want to communicate.

But how can a boy be friends with a beetle? And what does a beetle have to do with the disappearance of his dad and the arrival of Lucretia Cutter, with her taste for creepy jewellery?

A darkly funny Dahl-esque adventure.
KATHERINE WOODFINE

A wonderful book, full to the brim with very cool beetles!
THE GUARDIAN

Paperback, ISBN 978-1-910002-70-4, £7.99 • ebook, ISBN 978-1-910002-98-8, £7.99

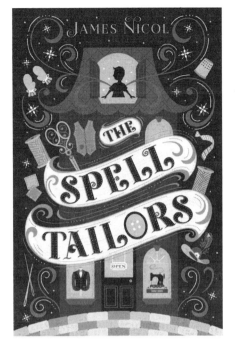

THE SPELL TAILORS by JAMES NICOL

Hen dreams of joining the family spell-tailor business, making magical handmade outfits.

But the shop is struggling, thanks to the cheap clothing factory that has opened nearby.

Stumbling upon a stitch – one that can sew memories into seams – Hen thinks he has the answer that will save them. Instead, he's shocked to be banned from sewing for ever.

What is going on? And can he unravel the mystery before it's too late?

A cosy, magical adventure which touches on the problems associated with fast fashion.
THE BOOKSELLER

Paperback, ISBN 978-1-913322-86-1 £7.99 • ebook, ISBN 978-1-913696-85-6, £7.99